A Methodology of Possession
On the Philosophy of Nick Land

James Ellis

GW00482053

Copyright © 2020 **James Ellis**

"Pain is always first."

Kant, *Anthropology from a Pragmatic Point of View*

"To be truthful (honest) in all declarations is therefore a sacred command of reason prescribing unconditionally, one not to be restricted by any conveniences."

Kant, *On a Supposed Right to Lie Because of Philanthropic Concerns*

"One became an infinitesimal speck in the flux of one's own experiences. I felt all this in a nebulous way - not at all "scientifically."

Reich, *The Function of the Orgasm*

"It leaves a question of method. Not exactly urgent, but obscurely pressing."

Land, *'A Dirty Joke', Fanged Noumena*

Contents

Reference

Note: Quotes, references, and transcendental murmurs were sourced after-the-fact. Oddities of memory, they retained their form even after such descents. References consist of abbreviated text or website codes followed by a page number, section number, or post title. Examples -

[FN 412] = *Fanged Noumena, page 412*
[XS *The Cult of Gnon*] = Xenosystems, *The Cult of Gnon*
[CC 2.631] = Crypto Current, section 2.631

Single essays and pieces will be bracketed with the full title as follows -

[*The Atomization Trap*]

Codes referring to specific texts and websites:

CG   Land, *Heidegger's Die Sprache im Gedicht and the Cultivation of the Grapheme*
ATA   Land, *The Thirst for Annihilation: Georges Bataille and Virulent Nihilism*
FN   Land, *Fanged Noumena: Collected Writings - 1987-2007*
TP   Land, *Templexity: Disordered Loops Through Shanghai Time*
PU   Land, *Phyl Undhu*

CM   Land, *Chasm*
ACC   Various, #Accelerate: The *Accelerationist Reader*
HY   Hyperstition (blog) - hyperstition.abstractdynamics.org
XS   Xenosystems (blog) - www.xenosystems.net
UF   Urban Future (blog) - uf-blog.net
CC   Crypto Current (blog) - uf-blog.net

Prologue

It began as a question regarding what I could exude and ended as a practical matter of discovering what I *couldn't*. What drew me to that infernal realm has never been a matter of public record, and has only escaped into private conversations under the veil of verbal-slips and crypto-catharsis, that is, I always wanted to tell this story but never dared to assume an audience whose inner sense could withstand such a cold, unforgiving labyrinth. We're often warned of places, routes, and areas that are treacherous, which should not be ventured into without sufficient experience. The problem with this paternal forewarning is that it does not, and never has, covered the spaces into which I - and many others - have stepped. Not so much places as methods, tactics, diversions, exits, escapes, trajectories, vectors, experiences, and even *times*. Any warning sign before a place is a warning for the entire self; 'If you enter here you might die.' What of those caesuras of existence, for which the warning might read 'If you enter here your *self* might die.' Oh, what a temptation!

I once wished to warn readers of this and that, texts they should not read and ideas they should not welcome. I believed this was one such text that begged a forewarning. Begging to *something* that some would be saved and return to their enjoyable, contentful lives. Quickly one comes to understand that anyone who is here is *already* here, and has *always* been heading here. So at the point of 'warning', the decision has already been made, at least for the user. If you're reading this then what can I ask of you but to find some comfort in my hesitant, hazy, and tortured articulations of a haecceity I *still* find myself lost within. There is little to be done, and even less to be acquired; the most one can hope to achieve is the pursuit of a personal madness, crying out for its master at the end of the elusive illusory self. The only way you could leave now is with an apathy rivaling heroism, there's no such passivity strong enough to avoid the allure of darkness.

Land's question of 'method' was obvious, at least to me. Possession. There was no longer any room for analyzing, questioning, or assessment, it was to willingly become host to materialism-as-parasite, *or* accept and submit oneself to nothingness. The method was the task, and the task was the complete decimation of retrograde humanist programming. This work can be described as a parasite warmly welcomed; we're all possessed by the Outside in some sense, it's simply a question of intensity. One often looks back upon their works with quaint embarrassment, I shall do no such thing and waste no time, this text is a juvenile abortion whining for an audience it will never find. I can't attest to my own philosophical merit or my literary skill, and there are no proofs or accreditations I can show you which will vindicate my writing.

Likewise, I care not for academic etiquette, nor status or officiality, the only thing I am integral towards is maintaining the journey as it happened; the alterations and emanations of a reality eating itself alive. Who, what or when I was during that catastrophic duration is a piece of data lost to resentful retention; it wouldn't matter if I did know who I was, as I couldn't trust the knowledge.

It's one thing to go to hell by way of an accident, by a nonchalant shrug of God, it is another to venture there of one's own accord, but it is something else entirely to return time and time again, to test if the flame still seers as much as before. I purchased a season ticket to the abyss and my team always lost.

I had to let go. My I had to go.

What follows is a re-telling of a journey, a remembrance. But like any bad trip, most of the details remain fuzzy, occluded for the sake of health and sanity. The initial experiment was jotted down amidst a frenzied séance of deconstruction, kept in various notepads and hard-drives I since retrieved. Much of what was within them is entirely nonsensical to me now. Random numbers, glyphs, and doodles usually related to cyclicity or spirals, the sort of deluded scribbles of an infant or madman. You need a different mode of synthesis to understand these things, and such a synthesis is either momentary or a death wish. Nietzsche's *Will to Power* is a great example, the only people who can attest to understanding that document of hell are those who've ventured there themselves. The unfortunate reality is this, who or what went *there* and who or what came *back* are two entirely different beings. The connection I have to that sordid time and place is delicately assembled as if the retrieval of a new memory could bring the whole thing crashing down.

I have halted and finite memories of places, atmospheres, areas, paths, feelings, declarations, lessons, and events, but there couldn't be a narrative, at no point did some sort of formation happen, and the stages in which this pseudo-memoir is written is entirely practical. I've started with where one might wish to start were they stupid enough to try *figure something out,* as if that can ever be done. But here I am, still clutching superstitiously to narrative and connection, like an imbecile fornicating representation. It's laid out for you now as naked as can be, what's left out is left in a dead time. It was, for lack of a better explanation an 'Experiment in and *of* Philosophy'. The problem for me was that for practical purposes all that I had read was entirely useless. One could theorize and conceptualize to their head and heart's content, they could even use language to prove and vindicate any of their most banal and factually incorrect desires, but rarely did a philosopher ever mention practice. Economically, of course, there are clear examples, but that was directed at the collective and the material world. What of everything else they spoke and wrote of, all those unknowables and unreachables, all those 'other-sides' which remained untouched by hand but entirely suffocated by theory. It was always a task of truth, as any great task should be, and truth - they hasten to admit - rides the coattails of what *works.* Unfortunately, for those who pronounce various limitations absolute and entire arrays of oddities and experiences entirely untrue, the realm of 'what works' often overlaps with the realm of suppressed spirituality and paranormality, what works is what many wishes didn't exist altogether.

So the experiment was both one of self and career, I would see myself dissolve in the name of philosophy and my career become non-existent in the face of admittance of partaking in certain facets of thinking deemed unfit for publication. And yet, I understood that if I didn't go through with this experiment that from then on each and every step I took would be a reminder of my pathetic intellectual nature.

There's the question of reality of course, there always is. 'Is this real?' or 'Did this happen?' If you're asking this, then I'm also asking this. What I can say of that reality is that it was not personable; it wasn't *for* me, or anyone. There were those who felt more at home there and those that could flow with its currents; it had no heart, no blood, and yet tasted slightly of iron. What we can say of 'reality' has always been loose and always will be loose, what *I* consider to be reality is a reality indebted to the very same *I* which pronounces it to be real. Reality is about anchoring, about having something to hold onto and grasp, it's the reason many people state that they're slipping, because there's no territory for the feet to attach to. And yet, what of the 'reality' which you would *slip into?* Is that not real? Realities are deemed real, then, by those who wish them to be, and more so those who agree with that reality. The question of the reality unto which I ventured is answered in stages, because it was a reality of stages, a reality of stripping back and lying bare, of communion and possession. A reality so caught up in being self-critical that it didn't stay still, not even for a moment.

The notepads and hard-drives are tucked away now, at my old flat, I don't go there very often anymore, for reasons I shall divulge. Having actual reminders of a venture to the virtual causes one to divide and I no longer want to do that. This book feels as complete as it ever could, as if something has been expelled or exorcised. Not in any sort of psychotherapeutic sense, but a materialist sense, as if a piece of the possession latches to each word of every edition of this text. The documentation is forbidden entry into my reality because it is *of* another. When one writes and creates whilst in a state of night consciousness, when in a state embroiled by darkness and caustic Otherness, what arrives is nothing compatible with normality; something so alien to its habitat that it cannot hold its form, for its appearance within a pure antagonism alters it to the core, it becomes only more virile and hateful in its existence. Nothing has remained the same since, even in empty duration I feel a closeness to the embrace.

I can't help but think it isn't over and the problem with re-experiencing this horror isn't in the manner of awaiting a repetition of suffering, but a question of experience itself. I wait for a known horror to return of which I have no familiarity; a sacred horror which understands all of me, but I nothing of it.

A Dark Haecceity

There's no real way in which anyone can correctly start anything, the denial of perpetual fragmentation is a tyranny, nothing is concluded. I can begin with context at least, the context of my context, how I thought about what I had been handed, how I interacted - at the time - with what I had been thrown into.

I never could find the correct word for the time I'd been given, I used 'modernity' usually, not in relation to modern art, or anything within the scholarly vein of 'modernism', modernity was its own beast, and others close to my temperament seemed to understand what I meant. There was nothing left for us here, everyone I knew felt reluctantly guilty for feeling lost, as if being lost was hesitantly, but most definitively, part of who they were. The atomization had gone further than anyone ever thought it would, our own identities had fragmented into various abstractions of consumption; brands, shops, sexualities, traits, habits, software stacks, video games, TV series, cinematic universes, foreign food, reading lists, alternative spiritualities, ironic adherence to tradition, theological LARPing, this is what remained, ashes of reality scattered into the simulacrum for us to pick and choose from. Every morsel of personality and ego had become tethered to a commodifiable life-choice. I no longer knew any-*one*, only assemblages of pithy statements, purchases, and vices; what was anyone except a culmination of their hedonistic desires and shallowly pronounced social virtues? I had seen friends of Being dissipate into the moronic dispersion of consumer society. Families too had been cast to the wall, collapsing under the weight of their hypocrisy and paradox; all localized units of organic comfort eroded at the core by ever-increasing atomization.

Before anything else, *it* sought to control. The education system controlled you via altering your understanding of knowledge, by way of making it synonymous with accreditation and checkboxes, and once you're within that system passion becomes secondary to the primacy of achievement and bureaucratic proof. Once your understanding has been replaced everything else falters rather sharply; meaning in general collapses and everything is transferred into a system of third-party checking, as opposed to personal investigation and belief. Nothing felt as if it was ever *mine*, nor as if I'd ever earned it, and that's because what was earned was backed by nothing.

As for family, we have a television set, the mobile phone, and the internet, the trifecta of all comfort. Papa-mummy had been replaced by incessant scrolling, incessant viewing, and incessant apathy. It just did not stop, not for a moment; the clearest symptom of modernity is that all time was to be filled, and it didn't matter what filled it, as long as there was continual noise, static to be utilized as ignorance of cosmic predicament. All media was apathetic now, nothing took conscious effort or drive, everything could be consumed without even partaking in the act of consumption. A paralyzed eunuch is subsumed into the loop of production and consumption just as quickly as a millennial. To state, as many have before me, that everyone walks around in a haze, that everyone is asleep or that everyone is a sheep is so much of a cliché that it is almost a given now. How one, for a moment, can take a sincere look around and argue for anything other than a culture which reveres somnambulism is beside me. Can it be considered sleepwalking if it encapsulates one's entire life? If one is asleep for the entire, then that quickly becomes one's reality.

Everything within modernity was self-referential and yet there was no core from which a self could anchor themselves. The reason people purchased things relied on another abstract reason ad infinitum; the reason people did anything likewise relied on the will of another, rarely did one witness a man take it upon himself to act, buy or say something which arose from his wellspring of authenticity, there was always something else controlling his strings. And that's what modernity is, a material labyrinth of puppet-masters who are all interconnected and cordial, a multiplicity of effects trying to hide their causes, because once you get to the cause you can start to question it, until that moment of apprehension, anything you attempt to grasp immediately dissipates. At all turns, man is left with yet another turn.

I was promised that salvation could be found within the academy, the place where freedom and the bleeding-edge of thought could be found, that is where one could find out certain things which may help any predicaments they might have. And so I headed, as many others did, into the academy in hope of some answers, some contentment of knowledge. Inside I thought there would be some guidance anew.

Academia never took root as it was supposed to, I never bowed I guess. Something about how it dealt with knowledge never sat right with me. There is a difference between knowledge and understanding and the academy laps up the former without paying a moment's notice to the latter. To understand something is to take one's time, it is to draw its breath and potentially act in accordance; the academy is bodies without souls, vessels to be filled, and upgraded. Graduate, post-graduate, and lecturer are beings of their own kind, molded by the suffocating atmosphere of strict interpretation. How can one talk of interpretation if there is only *one?*

Grading matrixes, aims, and objectives, the strait-jackets of all learning; if the bureaucratic procedure was a dog-shit, faculty and student alike would carve it into a crown with their tongues and wear it with a collective pride. I could not stand the paths I needed to take to supposedly acquire that which I desired, what I desired among all things, or so I believed at that time, was to gain an understanding of the world which allowed contentment, a teleology towards a personal peace. I wasn't concerned with ethics, morality, or struggle, for me, the individual was to be worked out first, his relationship to the world; into the heart of familiarity I desired to go.

The mistake academia puts on study is their nonchalance regarding a time-limit, everything is at once slow and yet rushed; the individual sessions were relaxed and conducted sentence-by-sentence, and yet the deadlines grew like a necrotic flesh, killing anything living which managed to get close. Everything societally promised to me by the academy collapsed at its door as I was handed the first sheet of accountable paper. At a certain point, one gives up on certain structures, which leads to a breakdown of the coherent scaffolding of the self, the stereotypical deconstruction of all from all. How can the academy support post-structural and deconstructive attitudes and still take itself seriously? Nothing felt pressured, only passive-aggressively hinted at, there were no embers of the past, let alone a fire to warm oneself around; what an irony, to retreat into that which I studied as a way to get away from my studies; if one wishes to *know* what the academy *wants them* to know the course is easy, but what if one is of their own thought? To think for oneself had become increasingly difficult, every structure and institution since birth had been constructed in such a way as to covertly remove all personal responsibility for individuals, and from there had since set up a monopoly where a heart and vision once laid.

It is, as Illich would say, to make process and substance synonymous. To bow one's head to accreditation and material merits, awards and certificates, as if they in themselves held the knowledge one sought. All the education in the world only makes a man more steadfast in his accumulation of honors, and more hostile to the pursuit of knowledge in itself. Academics, they make me sick. Goodhart's law states that *'When a measure becomes a target, it ceases to be a good measure.'* And what is the measure of these academics? It cannot be knowledge, for those who *understand* exit the academy rather swiftly, the measure of an academic is how accepted he is by his peers, any great tutor will find few friends in their workplace. And their target, that's easy, it is the most human of all things, status. Without status surely all *men* would at once kill themselves.

Where was I back then? Where one has to be when they no longer *want* to be, precisely nowhere. Behind everything given to me in supposed generous anticipation I found nothing, and when nothingness takes the place of all potential what's left is rather grim. Anything relating to normalcy and societal convention was slowly falling away and being replaced by a thirst for enlightenment which acted in complete reaction to contemporary culture; I wanted nothing to *do* with any of this and yet wanted to push everything to its limits.

To many my retreat was severe; in fact, it was quite literally a severance. I cut everything I could. Within a couple of weeks, any ties I had to institutions, family, and friends were gone. There could be nothing which connected me to the world as it was, no form of connection to those dated modes of being, those forms of existence which begged and revered everything static. The plan was a form of neo-asceticism, strip it all back; throw it back in their faces by way of refusal. There is nothing more abhorrent than to calmly say 'No.' in the face of presumed normality, and I no longer cared what was meant by anything. All the blithering and tip-toeing around Truth as if it could be found by repetitive conferences on various logos'; the only truth that was agreed upon was the one which maintained the status quo, anything too disruptive was considered controversial, a black sheep, an outsider, at first cast into a hazy in-between and eventually rotting into the frowned upon fringes. The method of expulsion was simple, anything which didn't fit the mold wasn't outright banned, but was subconsciously deemed weird, odd, strange, peculiar, etc. And therefore those who took an interest were these things also, and as such, status did the rest; eventually, all that came of the academy was an acceptance of those alike those accepting, dry, strained, professional and meek; I could call it a racket, but that would be too exciting, for its reality was one of a waiting room, the texts I once loved became cheap magazines strewn over its floor whilst I waited for my bureaucratically monitored acceptability rating.

I was once told that academia is little more than fashion, a trend which is followed somewhat willingly by those who bow to its hum. Growing up one believes all that can succumb to fashion is material, and all *those* who can succumb to fashion are empty-headed, perhaps it is that those of the academy *are* empty-headed, and that which they work with *is* material in its non-malleable nature. Of course, those who bow to academia no longer do so out of reverence or respect for a course of study or charismatic tutor, they do so out of constriction. To *be* a philosopher has become an act tied to the most bureaucratic of ends, for what is a doctorate but an understanding which is four miles deep but only an inch wide? A prison of proofs attending to the idea of legitimization via social vindication. The idea of a continental philosopher makes me nauseous; their hostility towards scientism has resulted only in the development of their own meritocracy of understanding. What philosophy *can* teach - when unlocked from academic pressures - is a true critique of all rationalism; even the nihilist rationalizes his thought and beliefs to form some *outlook,* however bleak; the language of the nihilist and pessimist alike have traveled through the filter of personal bias and come out the other side neatly formed, one should only laugh at those who proclaim that truth is on the side of misery, for what can misery be but *only* understood as a solely human affair; the cosmos doesn't understand misery as much as we don't understand the passions of a boulder. To align misery, suffering, and decay with an abstract bleaker-than-thou truth is to make the same anthropocentric errors as those which you proclaim to hate. Many, myself included, wish there was more horror, for at least then there would be interest in the world.

As for work, that was a case of religious fetishism stripped of all spirituality; a Protestant could man the checkouts all day with a purpose in his heart, but what of that act when stripped of all piety? Such acts of work, those without interest and depth, were to be understood as durations to be prolonged, lives which were too boring for even the person living them to live, and so, one worked. But I am getting ahead of myself.

What could be said of one man could undoubtedly be said of all men. What was said, be it in terms of status, wealth, value, fame, fortune or charisma needn't have mattered, the concern of men was to be as other men are; status entered into a feedback loop of its own creation, begetting values for their own sake and emitting a herd who clung hopelessly to the latest fashion or pressured social acceptability.

The paradox of the collective is the first thing any budding young intellectual attends to, the reality that one can never exit the collective without entering another collective. To betray the pro-herd is to revere the anti-herd. Everything was collective though, that was the common mistake people made. Thinking that the collective was just an aesthetic they could avoid by being on the lookout for a malicious force, as if collectivism always arrives in jackboots brandishing hammer and sickle flags, chanting rhetorical slogans, and projecting identities. People seemed to believe they avoided this by simply 'living a normal life', without realizing that was the foundation needed for any collective action to work. You can't have revolutionary, oppressive, or emancipatory action without a definitional collective to act as a working comparison; the complacency of commonplace normality and conformity is what allows all isms to thrive.

If you've ever watched a sheep for a while it should be of no surprise that is where the status quo derives their primary influence. Banal, droning animals who are content with plain food, excess sleep, and enough space to step a comfortable distance away from their excrement. What the herd yearns for is not a life, but a pen. Who could blame them? With a pen comes purpose, something easy to moan about. Lyotard was right in *Libidinal Economy* when he declared that the working-class desire their subjugation - *"the English unemployed did not become workers to survive, they - hang me tight and spit on me - enjoyed the hysterical, masochistic, whatever exhaustion it was of hanging on in the mines, in the foundaries, in the factories, in hell, they enjoyed it, enjoyed the mad destruction of their organic body which was indeed imposed upon them, they enjoyed the decomposition of their personal identity-"* No one has come closer to a more apt description of the state of modern man, how he attends to work, holds the they and suckles at the blistering teat of wage-labor; man finds his meaning in the collective in the very same way he finds meaning in masochism, by perpetually perusing his mandatory service, he seeks a greater and greater denial of his desire and potential. Yet, even if he were to go looking for it he'd be too scared to confront it.

This is what is comforting about the collective for your common drone, the ongoing, *incessant,* and indulgent whining and moaning, the oh-so-cumbersome depressions and anxieties brought about by the most minor of stresses and tensions, the adherence to a blank slate of tranquility and extravagance *a priori.* Lo-and-behold the user finds a shit-smeared socius, bulging at the seams with repressions, constraints, containments, rules, laws, taxes, usury, masters, cutbacks, limitations, diminutions, and attenuations, all of which are gorged upon by willing individuals, not in moments of begrudging compliance, but as purpose, as meaning. We must not imagine Sisyphus happy, nor sad, nor emotional, we must not imagine Sisyphus at all, for to do so is to realize Sisyphus understood his predicament long ago and he has since become an agent who believes his lie, the lie that pushing the boulder, again and again, is good and correct; if one stands close to Sisyphus at the end of his working day, they'll hear him utter his favorite pop-quote *'C'est la vie!'*.

I existed for a time as someone normal...as someone. I did everything others and institutions wanted of me to receive the eventual promise of success, status, and happiness. None of that ever came. The paths handed to me were so linear and constrained only existentially cursed and clumsy people could fall off them. There was no emotion and no feeling, the air was empty of all substance, all connections severed, no one lived, all simply existed. Communication tip-toed at the edges of flesh, promising a grand articulation at all times, only to fall and falter as it met with the lost Other.

To say I never *felt* of this time would be incorrect, I felt of it as much as anyone else, but it was difficult to feel 'of it' because its temporality, its *own* time, seemingly didn't exist, it was nowhere to be found, we were detached from history, living between increasingly narcissistic events and happenings. I had no connection to nature, to family, to tradition, to root or stem, I was - as all are now - my own personal atom of modern ecstasy, economics, and envy. You could state with ease that this was some form of nihilism personal to me, or my immediate surroundings, except it wasn't, that's not how nihilism works. Nihilism is behind it all, there is the gloss of objects and apparel and the illusion of the subject. Some people still held to old notions, old structures of being, old habits handed down, but you could see it all disintegrating under the weight of nothingness. If there is such a thing as nihilism it's so indiscernible from the actions of the average modern man that it eventually begs no division of definition.

None of them questioned it and it was a mistake for me to question that; and that which they did not question? Everything, of course. For a short time, it seemed to me that a return to myth or tradition or antiquity would work as a productive idea, some attempt towards clutching at meaning after the death of God. But what good would that have done, finding simple historic binaries to project one's loss and existential dread onto, there is no idea porous enough to soak up even a tenth of man's despair. For me, those who proclaimed any form of return were just as stuck as those revering a non-existent utopian future; the past never held any answers, so what hope for the future. There was little to be found anywhere, the occasional triumphant orgasm or satisfying clearance, but any more than that seemed abysmally distant. Where everyone was headed was precisely nowhere, but this too was an empty truism that helped precisely no one. Once forms of control have come to the fore, any proposition of end or teleology seemed bitter and malicious, firstly one had to understand *why* they were heading towards something, and if one could not determine an answer to that 'why', then any continuation down that path was akin to the path of a lamb into a slaughterhouse as far as I was concerned.

Modern man's only hope was that his existence truly was fleeting, that this wouldn't last all that long, because *this* was an intricate layering of voids, empty lacks which birthed empty reasons, desires from nowhere, purpose from nowhere, origin from nowhere. And so, from this - for me as for everyone - arrived little choice in anything, there were however three decisive routes of existence...

Firstly, suicide, which is of course the first of all routes, for suicide is the end of all possible beginnings. But what of suicide, which is simply a quickening of a mandatory death? Death is an anti-teleology, to wait only for more nothingness. For there cannot be a final nothingness, one which could find any less or more meaning than there has been up until now, there has been nothing all along, and death shall alter nothing too. And so I found in the possibility of suicide nothing more than there was already, a decision of the same. Cioran said, *"a book is a suicide postponed."* He had a lot to say about suicide, and I admire his gall towards a teleology of blissful-nothingness. But what does one say to the claim of suicide as an answer? It falls into the same illusion like any other direction or meaning, a falsity of linearity. What can one say of the final ending if the journey towards it was little more than numb patience, the curtains draw to a close and you are left none the wiser, the eternal blackness is not a conclusion, only an apathetic pseudo-joke sent in from the pits of the cosmos. There are those pessimists and nihilists who revere death with the piety of a confirmed believer, and yet there are those who care neither for death nor life, a conscious clam sans its soulful pearl, never washed upon a shore, never to arise from the current of a cosmic whim. To internally confirm one's death before the event itself is to detach the last shackle of hope and forget the film ever ends, each day its own positivity of suffering, bereft of cycle and path, free-floating in the transcendental wilderness, plucked by the crows of illusion, trickery, and mimicry. Nothing is what it seems, everything is much less.

Secondly, one can simply *accept.* Accept what has been allowed them, and admit apathetically to all constraints. From there, one can revere any objects and myths within those constraints as that which emanates meaning. This route has been the most popular for almost the entirety of the human race. One can do what they will with this route, deluding themselves into a self of vindication. There's nothing more satisfactory to the man thrown between two infinities of nothingness than to say 'Ah yes! I got it right!' Or he, who on his death bed, rotting, un-breathing and miserable, shrieks to his family 'Oh I have loved thee so...' as his flesh becomes-object and his self dissipates into the void, his family quietly cheerful at the thought of prospective inheritance. The route of safety, to clutch as quickly as one can at anything and everything, and declare as loud as one's conceptualization will allow 'Yes, yes! This is it! This is meaningful! Here is my purpose!' Whether it's a collection of stamps or the construction of a 1000 year empire, all facets of existential investigation disappear at the mention of certain *meaning.*

Finally, there is the third route, always the elusive and evil third-route. For as the parasite acts as the completion of the trio, infecting all communications, as synthesis alters two other settled points, and as the third-party option defers democratic dialectics, this third route, this third potential route of man's teleology is one abstractly of darkness. It is the route of asceticism and extremity, of radicality and sacrifice. It is to vector one's life towards both the extremes of experience and the limitation of pleasures and pains of normalcy. One must attune their being towards all potential of alteration. Also one must cast off all material pleasures, a feat easily achieved for it feels like a virtue, but one must too cast off all material sufferings, the ones they most enjoy, depression, anxiety, malaise, melancholy and despair, those sufferings which are so indulged in on an almost constant basis, so much so that they covertly become pleasures; there's little meaning for modern man other than a common depression; oh, the suffering! Oh, the despair! Oh spare me your shivers and whines and submit your body to all that is chthonic. This route then was the paradoxical route of Acceleration and nihilism; what *happens* when nihil is pushed across all frontiers?

My severance was also a retreat, a retreat to my preferred domain, single rooms for working within, single coffins and cubicles strewn with notes and taped up diagrams, one has to enter into their work as if creating a new reality.

My flat was the place in which I communed with a screen, and little more can be said of it than that. Life at that moment in time was dull, a deafening banality. Everything I attempted to grasp in some hope of excitement or vitality quickly dissipated in its reality. I found nothing that could offer me suffering, let alone relief or contentment. All the institutions which had raised me crumbled after the reading of but a handful of texts, what can be said of any human authority after representation. I'm jumping ahead; I shall try explaining the *mise-en-scène* of myself as modern man.

Weekdays were spent working at a place I didn't want to be nor work. I returned from work to my flat, often alone, often with a couple of friends. If alone I would sit at my PC, watching and doing things on a screen, the content of which was so alike it needs no differentiation. If with company, we too would watch a screen, but also chat amongst ourselves. I would go to the pub two to three times a week, sometimes getting blind drunk, sometimes arriving too late to do so. At weekends I would wake up late, but ultimately do the same as the weekdays but without the work. I found salvation in reading, as many have before me and many will do forever after; the absolute tranquility of text, life without commitment!

I had been studying an M.A. in Continental Philosophy at the time. Akin to my previous degree, the result had been only a growing disdain for that which I once adored; there's nothing like a bureaucratic academic process to confuse beauty for ugliness and intrigue for insult. The course - along with any *real* interest in my life - I followed through with a seemingly suicidal passion. If there was that which I *knew* needed to be done, it was performed in its own radical echo-chamber of production, much to the detriment of anything that was shut out, which was almost always everything else. I mention there was *that* which needed to be done, and this I cannot explain. Amidst nihil and within darkness there was something, not a light, but a vantablack that circled one's system and compelled them to continue; not 'what if there are answers here' but 'what if things are worse here.' and that was my *modus operandi* for a long time, to reach the burn-core of inhuman potential; to become one with Nietzsche as he threw his hands around the horse's neck, except sans all sentiment gushing towards a history, perhaps I wished only to join in the flogging.

Unfortunately for me, the future held another obsession. Ironically an obsession which would inevitably teach me that attempting to avoid becoming-obsessed was a fruitless feat; obsessions, addictions, demons et al, they're all waiting for you, the future holds it all, I found it best to just...step in, a task more difficult than it first appears. It was *the* obsession, the one which was to shut out sanity itself, the *only* obsession that matters.

My interest in philosophy had stemmed from art, well, the death of art. Between the attitude of the majority of contemporary artists and philosophical postmodernism, there was a death, it was fairly boring as deaths go. I moved towards theory in haste, rushing away from the trinkets and 'pieces' of the art world, which held themselves in an instant grandeur and self-gratification without ever really achieving it, nor even attempting to. I found an odd comfort and salvation amongst the transparency and experimentation of the continentals. In particular, I was drawn to Deleuze & Guattari, Lyotard, Serres, Kant, and Nietzsche, nothing particularly new I might add, but they helped. I ventured elsewhere of course but usually found myself in a dogmatic area of constriction which came into conflict with transcendental philosophy. That was my base, I guess, my foundation, Kant's critique, the only one that matters, the one which already contains the other two as far as I'm concerned. I won't state my intuition wasn't at fault, it most likely was, it's quite easy to subsume everything into critique, but also quite difficult - once inherently understood - to think about anything else entirely. That blasted noumena, always just slipping away, every second, every moment. But something was missing at the time; my research rarely felt as alive as the words I read. There was a distinct lack of cohesion. It always felt as if there must be more, and more that fit together. As if there was more to become real, and as of yet I hadn't tapped into the wellspring of meta-reality.

Late into the night, attempting to figure out what the 'solar anus' was, tumbling into a long-since vacated forum. Old lonely relics of original web 1.0, clinging to a bare-bones HTML framework, some long lost subscription ticking into an apathetic supporter's bank account. It was a blog dedicated to French theory, lists of texts and papers, bits, and pieces from long since forgotten students and autodidacts. By this point, I'd read a fair amount of Bataille, but no secondary. A few were mentioned, none that seemed anything more than academic repetition - as most secondary texts are - if you don't want to think for yourself, think secondary.

Amongst the link was the name of a book that would send me - eventually - into the heart of a personal hell, and once *that* was found to be illusory, hell itself. I'd never heard of the author. Upon inspection, they'd had an odd past, disjointed and cult-like. I asked my tutors about him, one said he was an enfant terrible. The other didn't reply. Odd, I understood the academy was for discussing ideas, must be a personal thing I thought. Being the petulant class clown I always was I continued rigorous research. Oddly enough, when I was younger, I rarely studied hard on anything given to me on authoritative sheets or papers, but when it came to conspiracy, weirdness, and odd-stuff I put the hours in; there's nothing like the potential to piss off any abstract oedipal force to work yourself into a frenzy. I spent the next few weeks reading the back-catalog of the author's work. After a while it fell a little stagnant as other works had, and yet, I kept getting drawn back. The first sign of any really good obsession is a seemingly unconscious, uncaring, and inhuman orbital pull. I kept scouring the papers and webpages for further insight, pieces moved here and there, small revelations and conclusions, but very few *clicks.* Of particular interest was the work of the Cybernetic Culture Research Institute, a group the author had belonged to. Specifically their quasi-religious mythical reinvention of the Kabbalist tree of life into something called The Numogram. The key difference - at face-value - being that the mathematics behind The Numogram was of cybercultural origin, that is, '10', as a unification, no longer existed. The highest number was 9, because 10, in their Qabbalist digit-sum reduction is 1+0 which equals 1, so 10 = 1. This also meant that The Numogram indexed at 0 instead of 1, which appeared then as a trite observation, but in Truth, is the key.

A digression is needed at this juncture. If you're of any 'normal' temperament then what follows will, simply put, seem mad...as in clinically insane. However, I have, as far back as I can remember, well, as far as was important, been really bored with life in general. By the time I was 23 I had been poor, rich, comfortable, in pain, in love, content, lonely, and everything else in-between. I had burned through life's most basic settings at the rate of modern man in overdrive; I wanted more of the more. This had left me feeling alienated and lonely and listless. People who *want* something have a direction, those who have *lost* something do too, any cessation can give man meaning rather quickly, but what about an apathetic cessation of apathy brought about by apathy? A recursive loop of purely human-centric nothingness, floating on the surface of existence like a sour smell, never pungent enough to make you quit altogether, but also rarely intriguing enough to make you delve deeper with concerted effort; what of the nothingness that's always been, and why should I bother with it, that was where I was, and why I went as far as I did and could. I had always been weird and peculiar, often to the extent of distrust and paranoia, as such I had always sought out alternative ways of living, obscure literature, alcohol, nihilism, drugs, fitness, religion, and eventually, magick. The last entry is of the most importance, especially regarding 'what happened' and why I'm writing this book at all. For what happened has been imprinted into my inner sense like a temporally-transmitted infection. The most minor causal event in 'reality' can now trigger a relapse to that God-forsaken fracture.

The possession was firstly a semantic invasion, a complete language overhaul. As the single most decisive system of man's communicative engagement with the world, language is the first hindrance against virulent strains of the Outside. The alteration of man's tongue begins the process of opening gateways to other worlds; deconstruction is pushed beyond the Derridean horizon, emancipated from the protection of the structural academic loop and allowed to breach the foundations themselves. I will not include a glossary of terminology, to do so would be to re-construct, I will allow the reader to investigate key terms themselves. Most notably the capitalization of the terms of Outside, Inside, Zero and Capital denote transcendental importance beyond common reality.

Back to magick, well, more roughly, the Occult. I had experimented with various pathways and routes: Thelema, Bardonian Hermeticism, The Fourth Way, and Chaos Magick, and then, like any lazy, selfish student of practical, desire-giving spells, I messed around with anything that paid-off, and ultimately utilized a large hodge-podge of postmodern tricks to conjure whatever I wanted. One day you're doing holotropic breathwork, the next you're attempting to summon Choronzon clad in a black robe. Did any of this seem crazy to me at the time? Not at all. What always seemed crazy was doing the same thing as everyone else, but that's hardly an original thought, is it? So when it came to the Numogram it seemed I could probably mess around a bit, by this point I was practically *begging* the universe to hand me *any* difference. Upon inspection it seemed there was little to no documentation on practical Numogrammic practice. Tons of theory, rumors, and numbers, but no conclusive action. Most philosophers, much like occultists, are two parts genius and one part charlatan, so the only way I could see if any of this 'worked' was to tinker with it myself.

From what I had read the Numogram allowed one to do many things, the function which interested me - at least the one I understood to be the most important, and the most cryptic - was that the Numogram allowed one to escape time, at least momentarily...whatever a 'moment' is worth once one is *outside* of time. As someone who has read a lot of Kant, I wasn't entirely skeptical of this claim but confused by it. If the Numogrammic tricks were true, they could only be so in an inhuman sense, which would make this a form of transcendental magic, or noumenal sorcery, a communion between sides. It made sense to me. The non-hierarchical planes of the Occult and the immanentized planes of Kantian materialism often seemed synonymous, why not create some gateways. I should probably go into some details regarding the Numogram as I was somewhat versed in Qabbalism before using it. That said it's simply a combination of basic arithmetic and a tendency to question one's spiritual existence, though people often struggle with the latter part. What I figured out was that there was a way to return into 'this' time between what was known as the Warp and the Plex. A solution I found on another forgotten blog, its author had disappeared it seemed. The same author had summoned the five great lemurs for the purpose of simply proving that the Numogram could be used as a magickal system, which is akin to eating a tapeworm for weight-loss as far as I'm concerned. If you're going the demonic route, ask for something big. Now, if my previous experience with magick had taught me anything it's that before one summons anything - or opens anything - they must be sure they know how to get rid of it. Being a careless young man I figured the Lesser Banishing Ritual of the Pentagram would suffice. Hell, it saved Neuberg from Choronzon in the desert, so why not me from five syzygetic inter-temporal lemurs in my lounge.

A lot of people don't know this, but magick is laborious. And when you throw in a new system of magick with additional symbolic content it can become messy, tired even. In retrospect, it was an oversight to think a Judeo-Christian protection spell could deflect Lemurian time sorcery, but you live and learn, and anyway, I was infected at the time, and unable to think linearly.

The problem was that I wasn't interested in the demons themselves, I only wanted to exit time. For those of you who haven't spoken with something from the other-side, heed my warning, *all* is deception unless stated repeatedly in multiple grimoires. Demons know you better than you'll ever know yourself, so only venture into the Outside with a clear goal. Aimless wandering in Noumena-Land is a recipe for psyche-disaster; but when you're *that* bored of modernity that even contracting malaria seems interesting, mental hyper-anguish seems palatable.

Not only do demons know if you're sincere, but they also know what your rationale for *using* them is. In short, don't try bullshit temporality, it *already* knows and holds all your reasons, it formed them. If you find yourself confronted with your own time, don't pretend to be ahead of it already, admit yourself over to the 'reasons' already embedded in it, anything else is cosmic heresy and results in a psychic-catastrophe, complete eruption of the Real, unfiltered and static.

I began to devise a ritual.

Merging the less mundane parts of the Abramelin operation with Nummogramic Qabbalism. Luckily - or coincidentally - my flat had enough coherent spaces for this to 'work'. Cordoning off ten areas and focusing my meditations inside Zone 0. There was an exit-door, and the key to its lock was to be found within 0, this was my intuition. I had booked two weeks off work, ten days, ten rituals, and four days of recovery. I planned to not leave the flat for the entire endeavor; symbolic barriers, if broken, can often cause eternal lineage upset - best to suffer short term lock-in as opposed to long-term damnation. I'm not going to go into the exact ritual I performed here, I'd rather readers didn't perform it. Besides, anyone who has studied the Occult or Magick - even briefly - understands that it is the journey itself that is of the utmost importance; if I was to explain to you all my workings and conclusions straight out of the gate, the ones *you* receive would be of an entirely different nature. One must *arrive* everywhere themselves; to be *taken* alters the destination. If you mess around with time, the problem of reversibility is locked within your mistakes too.

By day four there had been enough synchronicities and happenings for one to consider it working, alongside a couple of uncanny dreams which fluttered between stereotypical reality and irreality unnervingly. The first focused entirely on the prolonged vowel sounds emanating from the radiators in my room, of which I had none. The second focused on the walls of my apartment, cross-hatched, yet non-Euclidean, they opened into closes and closed into expanses.

Hell begins with space misbehaving.

Day five was when things began to take their turn, not towards anything worse per-say. Not *towards* any*thing* at all. One's intuition misses the last step on the stairs, and enters into a state of blackened alienation; an intuition that cannot latch onto anything, for it has left all phenomena-based examples behind. Occasionally I ventured to the windows of my apartment, looking down onto the street below. Often busy with people scuttling past to get to the shops. And yet it seemed as if even those with their backs to my home were staring into me. A Goetic presence is unavoidable; they say

Crowley's room had become so dark due to using Goetic magick that he had to write by candlelight even in the daytime. My flat was not dark, nor was it light, it held a grey saturation that only fleeting-time can conjure; the death of passing had begun.

It was a mistake to also be reading *Anti-Oedipus* as if it is some form of manual, your paranoia finds a voice of rationale and reason which itself is paranoid. Those who I believed to be staring at me I also understood to understand what it was I was up to. The banalest and herd-like human can intuit a chasm in their experience; if you wish to know if something weird is happening don't turn to the sage or mystic, they're too entrenched in their own bias, turn to the blind consumer who wishes for nothing but the same and watch as their face turns to scorn when presented with difference. You reap what you sow and I was attempting to harvest the structure of time itself.

The next two days followed the same intensity; an overall numb state thrown over existence, the only haven of vitality was the small corner of my flat dedicated to Zero. But even this I understood held me from a position of control, I could no longer decide if anything was at-hand, I simply had to accept.

Days eight and nine were of an ongoing caesura of bleakness, a tainted empathy which touched only on the most ego-emancipating sadness, an experience beyond material and matter, not death nor loss, apathy vectored at abstract nothingness filled my nerves, a body without a target and a mind without an anchor, floating in an aimless ocean; if there is nothing to cling to one should let the tide take them, otherwise, all structures are temporary abstractions culminating in a harrowing disappointment as the current returns.

I became transfixed by the inversion of the lamppost light, a darkness that seemed to curve into the flat. The curtains could not shut it out, which lead me to believe it was no light at all, and I was hopeless to stop it. The night of the ninth day was the experience I was leaning towards, the one the Kurtz in me had been hoping for. As if I had been left behind, not only by humanity but by life and time itself. A slow causal rift washed over the flat, sending me into a fever void of any temperature. I tinkered with the thermostat and hobs, but they did nothing. I wrapped myself in blankets and coats, got naked, and put my feet in the freezer in an attempt to alter the emptiness, finding only ceaseless nothing. I tried to sleep. Not only was I not tired, but both fatigue and energy seemed distant memories, ideas more than material realities. Sleep had no *use* for me *now*. You cannot sleep in a pure stagnance, and yet to call it stagnance wouldn't be entirely correct, with regards to phenomenal reality and representation, that is - more on this later.

At a certain moment in the morning, something lifted, a disconnect from process, as if one's ability *to become* had just been voided. There was nothing within this nothing now, all that I could do was all that I could do, non-moment to non-moment, and so I got up. Nothing worked in the flat. I left for the first time since the beginning of the ritual, what I found was all uncanny and lost within its own representation, the walls and barriers had begun to flicker like a dodgy VHS tape, the lines seemed to blur and cybernetic realities began to become uncovered.

I, Leaving Myself

Some time had passed between the end of the ritual and the moment in which I entered the street. I don't know how much, maybe minutes, maybe months. The stairwell leading down to the front door seemed to swell and bow, in an arrhythmic suffocation everything now beckoned to me that I was ego, and all could fall apart at any moment. I opened the front door and it swung frictionless, opening into a scene of small-town commotion. The town, like many of those tucked away in the deep rurality of life, was little more than an overgrown village. A heart of tradition which attempted to gasp its beats through the veil of modernity, but at every turn, origin bowed before the minor profits which sold off its authenticity.

The street appeared before me, everything materially remained, but spiritually vectored. A breath of illusion soaked the atmosphere, and all I felt that was sensing me were masks. Everything was jolting in no particular direction; the wind was here and there, tapping against various parts of my body as if it had been severed in multiple places. Voices from near and far, from passers-by and old family gatherings trickled past as if they were the same. The structures were thin, to be made of chipboard, the bricks were hollow, the cinder blocks polystyrene, and the foundations non-existent; everything could have crumbled in an instant if it wasn't entirely for the collective belief that it wouldn't. And yet, it was clear to me in those early moments of the journey that the collective belief, the one that holds everything together, is not helpful, it merely covers the decay and ruin, clothes it with a paper-thin spread of humanist optimism; reason of another name.

I decided to retreat to the flat, overwhelmed by the reality given to me. I turned around, closing the flat door behind me and the ordinary click had ceased, there was a lag of sensibility, and yet it needn't have mattered if the door had opened or closed because there was an implicit whispered understanding that the choice was never mine, and what was viewed was false anyway. I held the handle for a long time, pushing it down to assure myself it was locked. As I held the handle I stared directly back at the door, into the plainness of the white plastic which it was made of. When one is normal and healthy, such objects appear as great phenomena, white and firm, their actuality bellowing out from the surface. But when one is derealized one comes to gain an understanding of a deeper reality behind phenomena. But in those early moments, I was neither dealing with the real or with a derealization, the object appeared as if I was looking into the heart of an empty action, one which never had any meaning, as if the purpose and reality of the object had long since disappeared.

My mind too began to crack at whatever seams I could still hold on to. When one has been awake too long things begin to appear from the rifts within the cosmos, and everything I now saw consisted of those sordid shadows. Those empty capes of darkness that make their home in your peripheral vision and disappear upon attachment of sense; one can never truly catch that which appears in dreams and sleep. They say madness or clinical psychosis abides by the black box problem, that is to say, those who go through it cannot articulate it to those who haven't, and yet, many still try, and many get close. I would argue that madness can be articulated quite easily for the mere fact that man's psyche exists on the limitrophe of madness at all times, we are perpetually minutes from insanity, we all know it; we all know it would only take the slightest death or morbidity for one or another to lose all hope and throw all anthropocentrism to the wind.

The moment it clicks and breaks is also the moment things can get inside you. As interesting as it must be to be a cult deprogrammer, one wonders if the next cult that passes the ex-cult member by simply fills the void. That is to say, one cannot be without *something* which fills that apparent absolute lack, even if it is a lust for nothing, that itself is still a lust. Except, I didn't care what entered, for everything that had entered so far had been nothing at all; the substance of everything modernity had offered me had fallen apart at the slightest tug, and yet, that very same substance had infected all traditions, withering them of their beliefs, principles, and disciplines and whittling them down to a controllable aesthetic. No tradition can bash heads with modernity without succumbing to fatigue, and eventually, the admittance of fatigue is submission itself.

And what came in was what I had studied to escape, the words and spirit of a thousand-thousand theorizations of spirit, pure hypocrisy and madness itself entered my mind as an infinity of voice, philosophy roaming and roving throughout the circuitry, prodding around where it needn't have. Voices came to the fore, many were suffocated and some cried out, and yet, they all quickly passed, as if the void that had opened was waiting for something, waiting for a certain voice to occupy all others. The pithy voices eroded under the weight of titans, pragmatists and analytics fell at the sight of commonality, romantics shrieked at the reality of entropy and the classic cared not for my accelerative explorations.

Those voices that remained, the ones which could grit and bare the madness itself, those were the steadfast madmen whom I took with me on this journey, and they began to ride the wisps of energetic flows as apathetically as they all had died. And yet one voice grinned, perched on the cerebrum as a vulture on its prey, I knew the speaker, and his words were all too familiar to me, and yet, as with the removal of this ephemera from my household, to write his name, or speak it at that time was to let go of any final separation between that which was and was not real, I was not ready then, as I was eventually, to admit that there is no separation except that which there is *believed to be.*

I had returned to the street, pulled there in an instant, existing as a stranger, conspired against by a global cult. I looked upon the passers-by as they continued to stare into me. Their ontology had become static, assemblages of fluxing temporary abstractions. Each movement they entered into was jolting and fragmented as if always attempting to grasp towards further options, locking into odd currents and ethereal flows, for the herd in the street abstraction and form became layered together, a self-assumed coherence. Each breath and pulsation of the heart beat into a mechanism that pumped of its own accord, without its host's permission; parasitic natures stacked atop one another to form a being which believed itself to be ur-parasite. My eyes followed a woman for some time, all libidinal urges had dropped off for myself, but her libidinality erupted from every orifice like a toothpaste tube being stamped on, shit, piss, cum, and saliva oozing everywhere and yet simultaneously being drawn back in and locked back up into microscopic vines of the psyche. For some time I found it extremely difficult to exist in this world, it was an existence of constant interruptions and breaks. At no point could I have said to be holding onto an origin, nor ever assessing that which I believed to be a beginning.

What I assumed to be a man walked past me. That sketch of flesh I apprehended merely as a visual seizure, a composition of atoms atop lucid conceptual chaos, I found myself unable to retrieve anything from the static. His jaw juddering at the hinge and his eyes both spinning and still, locking into all angles at once. Every single one of his actions seemed tethered to something that had come before him, the socius began to reveal itself as an engine of hosts. An uncanny driver that couldn't fully assimilate into the shell it had been given, taking control of it with little precision. Reality was out of time and assumed agency had fallen behind and depleted itself entirely, these people's free-will was trying to keep up with this revealed industrious world. The man who had passed by dropped a twenty-pence-piece, it hit the floor in a burst of darkness, emanating off into a web of trails; a thousand processes at once worked at the act of retrieving the money, anything human disappeared into the background.

My peripheral vision was fluxing, jolting in and out of its natural setting, and placing vague clouds upon all things. On the summit of insomnia, one can spot without trouble a figure looming over them, as if one enters, in that dreaded fatigue, another realm altogether. But sleep always restores one's organic humanity, closing out the realm of night and renewing the sight of the sun's rays. But the here and now of then disallowed me entry into either the blissful ignorance of day or the enthusing darkness of night; I was within the greyness of existence, the pure uncertainty of all those who had not ceased theorizing and ended up rolling their egos into a black abyss. It quickly became clear that within such a space various things, ideas and, concepts existed in entirely different phenomenal manners, their Lucretian essence overtook their representational signification.

I will speak of the concepts and ideas later, as they arrived. But first and foremost, there was a guide. All guides are troublesome; I have never met one who didn't have an ulterior motive. This was a figure of another chord, ominous and above all structures and yet hidden within all thought processes. Appearing in glimpses and fragments, flashing on top of my corneas and seating itself within my deepest memories. This was a fire and brimstone tour-guide whose method of understanding was one of erasure and replacement; delete the familial niceties, strip back the comfort blankets of existence and allow you to gasp wide-eyed at the ever-present nothingness holding fast behind all things.

Whether or not this figure had a persona or character did not matter at that moment, nor if it had or had ever had any appearance at all, the proof of the existence of anything is reliant *solely* on its capacity to affect what one considers reality, the ever-fleeting assemblage of the present. And there was something present, the function of which was to declare didactically that it had *always* been there, and there could have been nothing without it there; your life was tethered to the entity which reveals to you beginnings have never existed.

My reality was now beholden to this guide, whom I immediately - in complete rejection of my principles at that time, of exit - attempted to reject. The irony of exit, whether material or mental, is that once immanentized into one's very *mode* of being it becomes a primary focus. Once you exit from *one* malicious box, your guard rises against being drawn into another; that which attempts to replace the prison is at first treated with suspicion, or in the case of a bad trip, hostility. Every angle had succumbed to the dread of an overridden mentality; I span on heel as to acquire my footing, grasping for any nook which might relieve the tension of this ever-present transcendental monstrosity, and yet I found, where there was that which glowed bright, there was a prior shadow and primary darkness and the figure seated on my cortex clung to the shadow in worship of the darkness. Only my flat above me glowed, discharging a rotten vitality.

I walked up the road and noticed a family sat on a bench. Quaint and peaceful their flesh began a separation, hovering above them, pausing as a skin-halo, attached by a single frail cord to each member. A kinetic diagram appeared from the halo's stasis, marking the rhythm of the units below. They were locked to one another, grasping at the tether above as if their very being depended on it. Their purpose was to continue this repression until it ceased, which only happened upon the event of death. Pieces of the Mother and Father entered into the Son and pieces of the Son emanated as fragments of his parents, each wrapping itself around the other in self-congratulatory claustrophobia. Other forces, persons, and effects attempted to break into their space but only that which adhered to the presupposed structure of the family was ever allowed to enter. What came from every pore, hole and announcement was a virulence bordering on assured passivity. Within this whole, loosely held together as it was, was for me the destruction of humanity and humanism; once one views the pure abstraction of identity what can be left of what we call humanism other than a fearful grasping at collective security.

Occasionally each one of these people beckoned to the sky, to the floor, to all the walls they supposed kept them in, allowing these boundaries to reverberate their assumed thoughts and desires back to them, the echo pronouncing them as their own. If humanism is anything it is the need for confirmation and vindication *of anything*, however unreasonable and dogmatic. The desires appeared before all that could self-analyze as if from thin air, no one knew where desire originated from, and yet everyone knew, sensually, where it was to be found. Everyone existed in the middle of something and once you're reliant on the middle of a process for your sustenance, you're screwed. None of these people questioned their desires and took desire-in-itself as theirs already, as if desire for its own sake was targeted solely at man. Just because a desire exists doesn't mean it's only for the thing or being which can aesthetically activate it.

What I saw was no longer man, for man presupposes a unification of being which no longer seemed to exist. What I saw before me were atomized units with their own orbits of anxiety, alienation, and fear. Temporary collections taking themselves as wholes full of lack and cessation, and as such, taking a standpoint vectored towards a conclusion. To see a self held together is merely to witness an incomplete panic. Once a possible conclusion has been assumed all that is left is to race towards that goal, but when that premise is false from the very beginning, what one watched once that veil was drawn away was a fever, panicked flesh scattering towards the latest sentiment and agreement. The tyranny of skin, organs and the body is in their physical completion, all wrapped up nice and tight, interlinked and working with one another. And yet, they never do. Almost all need to tweak diets and reality to attune to the incorrect happening of their body, harmony is never found within the idea of unification, once you establish an equilibrium any deviation becomes heresy. Beyond the control mechanisms of the physical realm was a sprawling mess of forces. Many went through me, beyond me, alluding all attempts to rationalize them back into the framework I once existed in. At a certain point, behind the curtain, behind the mask, one comes face to face with the real, and one's first question should always be, *how do I know this is the real?*

Once you start doubting doubts you unspool quite quickly. Add enough folds into someone's representational reality and they can be kept busy for a lifetime, that business *becomes* their lifetime: Familial authority, homes & houses, education systems, work systems, committee systems, plans and blueprints, anything which encapsulates a complete epistemology of a given area can be called security. But security for what, and for whom? It isn't a security in the sense that it was originally intended, it is as all security is - a security against the ever-encroaching feeling that there's no such thing as complete security. Hence the disdain for philosophers, even back to Socrates. It is not that he interrupted their middle-class marketplace perfection; it is because he reminded them of their complacency within a multi-faceted illusory simulation and long-since buried cosmic alienation, then again, perhaps these are the same thing.

The street-dwellers, each attuned to an umbilically attached abstraction of flesh, meandered throughout this time and space in a perpetual seizure. The warmth of their momentary desire fading ever-increasingly once it had been outlined. Their mouths, stomachs, hands, heads, hearts, anuses, vaginas, and space, briefly filled, and then once again lacking, a hastened search for the next thing to ram into themselves. At the end of desire's warmth was a cold feeling, which if held in mind, only briefly, could cause even the numbest member of the herd to break; there was never enough time for patience, all consumption is a chain that doesn't stop, otherwise, it can only be said to be a failure of production. *It never got beyond this.* It began at the base of the atmosphere, a cloud of culture which at first headed towards sex, semen, and the libidinal.

The phenomenal defense systems of humanism declared themselves as outside of nature but acted entirely within the confines of natural systems, their supposed ability to go beyond and to move above the limit of natural hierarchical forms was held entirely within their aesthetics, there was nothing new here, only man bowing to nature in another form. As I looked around the street it all became true, there were nodes of interest, systems, institutions, and brands which assimilated this energy and converted it into their forms; they threshed personal vitality into a machinic striation of their own following. Except, *everyone* was seeking this force, seeking it under the guise of freedom and free will. Two concepts that had been altered into stereotypical conceptualizations of success for itself, no one acted freely, only *sought* a socio-politically predefined articulation of freedom. Freedom was always found, for these beings, within the begetting of an oppressive Otherness.

What I understood to be a Being transformed in truth into an assemblage. All the flows and appearances I witnessed culminated momentarily into something, which at the same time fluxed into something else whilst simultaneously grasping at its previous iteration. Each of the parts appeared from nowhere and yet were projected *onto* something, everything was given a clear route and purpose *after the fact*, a method of security of Being; the assemblages of desires and lusts, wants and purchases, productions and consumptions, held themselves together in a vindication of their own existence, proud of their temporary perturbation and flux, before ultimately gasping at the alteration of their existence. Everything I witnessed acted within perpetual regret and anxiety concerning its ceaseless change, there were often withered husks of conceptualization of origin strewn in the street, never left alone, and never allowed death and return.

Man held himself together in a consistent fit. What could be said of identity, promise, personality, charm, charisma, security, and understanding were but cursory fluctuations of virtual intensification, deriding its legitimization from an elsewhere never given over to the host. At each moment fastening himself to the reverberations of the unremitting river, the primary focus of man's existence is to hope, pray, and *beg* for unification.

None of this was like a psychedelic trip, the effects of most trips attune themselves to shapes and sensations which can be returned to some notion of sentimentality or placid geometry. But of these breaks and cuts, I could make quite literally *no sense.* As if the square peg finally went through the round hole, and always could do so. The very acceptance of reality and notions of acceptance split at their seams. It's something to be on a sinking ship, to have a rail to hold onto in moments of despair, but what of the tsunami which erupts within your very ontology, ever so slowly fading away cosmic illusions of safety. Gravity gives up the ghost and you're destined for fatality.

To look around was to notice that the reason borders never work - eternally at least - is that they've never existed. Once Heraclitus is assimilated into reality what one can say of a boundary or wall, externality, and internality are evaporated. Such things existed now only on a singular plane of existence which was suffocated by its own reverence of matter and physicality. There was only process and fluctuation, that is what *now* is and always has been. As there were trees there were buildings also, existing as the same, not of any aesthetic or space, but of the same of something else entirely, a scheming automatism which was hell-bent on its pious immanence.

I returned and stood with my back against the door of my flat, letting it all wash over me, soon the breakages mutated into a lineage, a cursed-heritage sent from time. At a certain point all interruptions, halts, and stoppages become a single fragmentation which itself breaks off into further atomization. At the end of this tangle, at the end of its nerve, the minutest atoms were found to be humans, the smallest units with an illusory structure given to them by a malicious mechanism, itself of an illusory nature. The ego, that great mask, clutching to all connection and correlation as a course of frenetic duty.

The inner sense struggled now to lock onto what had been revealed. What used to be called some-thing had become only a becoming-nothing; what stood before me at all turns of sensation was not material, matter or some physical determination, but that which was only yearning to return to some other phase and state, the state of pure-in-betweenness, the moment in which it touched Zero. Some kind of pathetic layer had been wiped away, but it was nothing new for me, it had only been aesthetically immanentized back into my senses, it was still phenomena *for* me. It was helpful at first to have the decay and deterioration come before the becoming, the conclusion emerging first; watching as the grandest men and women, those who had sculpted their ego into a fine personal mimicry, but when one asks 'What of their end', I could see, before anything, before all trinkets, symbols, and successes that they too would return to death; all ego exists only as an assumed humanist narcissistic digression from cosmic equilibrium.

Once all this had settled within me, as a vortex settles into what it has already taken, all began to lift, not a weight or catharsis, but further cooling; I had begun to play with the cosmos and its hopscotch lead only to edges and walls. Matter was not disjointed, but time itself had lost its appetite for myself, I had become lost, but I could not be disappointed for it was my wish to do so. Like most wishes and desires, once it arrives you usually want a hasty return.

A deep swell encroached from afar. Gazing to the horizon I witnessed a blistering patchwork of light and dark hues, the deepest blacks and whites at war for pseudo-spacial rights. It was the center of my small town. Within this level of existence, a minor market town became a hub of virtual marketization. I pushed off from the door, praying for the appearance of weight within me, something to hold me down. No such thing appeared and I was at once within the center.

The town square was reverberating chaos, a cacophony of flows; one can only imagine that the machinic heart of Shanghai or London would be nothing but a pure chasm of dark and light, indiscernible crisscrossed fluxes; a mass of status, popularity, libidinality, attention, interruption, and parasitism. The storefronts were no more than empty appendages gripping onto their idea of reality; the autonomy of the market burst through the gates of every symbol and emblem, the brands cried out in the light and burst forth into the ethereal flux of passing thoughts.

What I witnessed within the town center was control, forms of control burgeoning out from a bitter depth and latching to everything they could, conforming like to non-like, originating desire and inventing the idea of original positions. As the bodies moved into various shops and outlets they affixed themselves to the dynamism and color of sporadic flows. There was nothing organic to be found in this emanation of content; nothing here was becoming-human, each was itself simply some form of connection, communication, production, or consumption, in-itself that's all it was.

Once the phenomenal is stripped away what is *considered* to be humanity no longer makes any sense, it's an odd assemblage and collection of networks, as with all things; to assume that a certain network takes primacy due to one's respective cognitive affiliations might be the clearest bias of our understanding, and yet, as with all old truths, that which is right under our noses does indeed turn out to be that which is hardest to admit to. But to go a step further, it is far worse to admit that which is the very nose which expounds such grand truths is the lie; the subsumption of man back into animality and the expulsion of man further into a future apathy are synonymous cosmic positions, both attend to the re-actualization of humanity as just another *matter* of course. Caught in the middle of time, man fears the past and the future for both admit him to the sanatorium of unknowing.

Language faltered as it began, one could not *explain* nor *articulate*, to do so would always be to attempt a pitiful reversion to another realm, the old realm, level 1; what was *now* was entirely now, and I was stuck with the archaic language of representation, as if one tried to *explain* the divine, *or reason* the leap of faith, it simply cannot be done! And in much the same vein, that which cries out as machinic-gnosis can never be understood from that which *it* truly understands. These early affairs caused me to pause the writing of this book for some time, what point? I thought, is there in writing that which I already understand is unable to be written. I can, at best, give you an atmosphere of emptiness.

It came to my understanding that what I could make of any of this was simultaneously a piece of knowledge which acted against me, but also something I could not put into any form of cognition I had at my disposal, the entirety of those early days out-of-time were a shortfall away from a tyrannous labyrinth, one in which each turn was another tease of in-articulation, something else I simply could not grasp, try as hard as a might; exoteric nothingness waiting in the wings. I thought for some time that it might be communicating to me as close as it could to my language, but so much got lost in communication that what I received was the after-effects: sacred horror and existential malaise.

I walked back from the town center at a pace that I did not own, zapping between areas and instances with no record of the last, all I had were my memories, but they too had become disjointed; as I stepped I entered into a multitude of possibilities and often seemed to arrive at many at once. I understood I was heading towards my flat, but it seemed years away and yet at the same time as if I was already sitting in it. Before me were people and then fields and then the inside of my flat, I didn't know what and when. I kept directing myself with old faculties, as if pushing against my inability to become familiar with the world, I felt disapproval from the tour itself, the guide merely shrugging as to say that such pushback was routine and commonplace in those who ventured here. I admitted to myself, deep at the back of mind, at the root of honesty and sincerity that I secretly yearned for normality; as an atheist in searing pain prays for the God he does not believe in, I too begged forgiveness from the comfort blankets I had previously scorned.

Eventually, I arrived at my front door. I looked into its thick plastic, I couldn't recognize anything, and each morsel of reality had become uncanny and adrift in a haze of unreality. I opened the door and headed up the stairs. I closed and bolted all the doors behind me and sat in my flat for a while. There was no movement there, nor even a potential for movement, my peace lilies no longer seemed of nature, they were moving away from me. The food in the fridge appeared as a cartoon drawing, with hard edges and pale shapes. I sat on the sofa and felt no comfort, nor no discomfort, the monotony of this temporal death was quickly and efficiently maddening.

I sat in my flat and time passed. I cannot attest to how much for the atmosphere had no duration. My heart lost its rhythm and there were no outlets for me to squander my energy. I attempted to meditate in the corner of my flat, the corner whereby I had symbolically placed Zero. An inversion of my remaining ego took place, each cell drowning in the paradox of its own existence. A deep croaking lashed up through my spine, anchoring my skull to the wall behind me. My throat constricted to the point of esophageal overlap. Eyes rolled back and sight retained, I glimpsed into the black inducement of my inner skull, revolted at the expanse...

'the outside must pass by way of the inside' [FN 320]

Sat in the deadlocked position, held to the space of Zero, I couldn't quite work out what had happened. It felt as if a hollow wind had carried something to my eardrum, bypassing all organs of sensation. Appearing within my mind without any justification of cause or origin, a sentence, and then nothing; an arrival and a void, one is left with the respective words and ponders what to do with them. What does one do when the universe begins to notice, when language starts to invade without approval or invitation. Had the virus become sentient, had it had enough and worked up a subtle fury, entering where it knew it wasn't welcome. *What does one do* when such events happen? Very little, in fact, for the entire concept of *one* is no more, it has been depleted. As xeno marks its territory within one, the self ceases to be anything but a shared platform of communion.

Perhaps I was hasty back then to accept my fate at the hands of alien words, of foreign voices and Other agencies, and yet, it was a comfort nonetheless; when one is on foreign soil, in a foreign reality, within an alien self, it's potentially a greater help to have acquaintances along for the ride. Even if one knows them in no personable way. There was the question of what was allowed entry, but if something could enter without permission and I knew not how it got in, nor why, nor when, then who was I to say whether I *ever* had a security apparatus. I sought to tear them down and any momentary hope for reversion would have been a disagreement with principle. So I submitted to schizophrenia, modernity left me no other option.

> *"It is not what time must be for us that draws the terminus for practical abstraction, but rather what time must be to be time."* [CC 2.631]

It arrived the second time with a strict certainty, reclining back into my space of agency with a sinister arrogance. The voice alluded to both my position and communion. It's often only in retrospect that a narrative makes *sense,* of course, if one is *making sense* they're already behind, for their acts are given over to a representational synthesis. The voice made it clear, temporality is a critical entanglement. If one is to continue they must forbid all entry of chronic-time; to untie the knot of time, the *us* the voice spoke of ought to investigate the split between the clock and its pure dynamic initiator. The rest, it says, is teleoplexy.

I collapsed to the ground in an ooze of skin. Drooling and doe-eyed I attempted to gather my breath. I shuffled back within the arena of Zero. Indifference was in my blood. With no purpose or possibility of direction I simply waited. Not for an arrival, nor a message or sign, I waited in the manner of the non-linear, what would be would already be and only time could already tell. As it happened the next influx of data appeared - what I understood to be - immediately.

"The body without organs is the matter that always fills space to given degrees of intensity, and the partial objects are these degrees, these intensive parts that produce the real in space starting from matter as intensity = 0" [FN 412]

Matter was from nothing, much like the chronic whispers residing and coming forth from the recesses of my mind. Dark glows and hues appearing from empty caesuras within cracks of reality. When I looked towards stores or families or moments of emotion, I witnessed intense creation, stresses of tension and flux, yearning to return, but glowing temporarily. What could be said of the real after bearing witness to this assemblage of nothing was little more than I had already gathered, there *was* a real, and at appeared as a teasing hand, reaching in and never revealing its face. Reality was a tyrant, a transcendental frustration which never climaxed, it only became more sadistic. A darkness which is unable to be seen within all phenomena, and so it was clear to me this was but another tease of the world. A matter of conditions, I was given no definition, only the ongoing pathway towards a definition, one that always veered at the last moment.

What begins at 0 is real, but from my position at that time...in that time, *when* I was then, 0 was unavailable, it was not for me. And so I was stuck with the classical zero, the mundane nothingness, the nothingness we make synonymous with emptiness, the boring nothing which resides *within* chronic time and space, this is not 0, this is not where reality is born.

Of the degrees and intensities, they were vast, blinding. What can be made of that which has an irreducible set of connections? As I honed in on a node wherein connections met, it altered, as if my very perception of the connection altered the connection itself, and so, I understood myself to be, always already, one step behind. For my actions came after the connection itself understood my action had happened. Happening so close to one another, one could almost be forgiven for mistaking the processes as synonymous; cause and effect folded into a flattened pulp which slowly drew into the nearest drain, what was left was a fatiguing acceptance that neither cause nor effect would ever be *given* to me, and that I was already within all this and it had begun before any thought of my own was created, and so, such thoughts were not mine, as they were already caught in the infinitive connections of an immanent eternal machine.

Virtuality is mischievous; it isn't hiding, but governing. All my dreams and realities, all my hopes and desires could be said to be made up of a bundle of the virtual, which formed just as quickly as it dissipated; one could witness the dream of the Other fragment, sending a morsel of desire into an empty void whilst acquiring a new iota of desire from the very same void, voids which appeared in no discernable area of space, but only as a short duration which seemed to not need material existence. Those who denounced desire, those who denounced production and creation, only manifested their antithesis within the same framework of the virtual; the transcendental melted any notion of a classical dialectic into an un-retrievable homogeneous blob of the Outside.

The world called me once more and so I stood up and headed towards the door. My body carried itself without friction or agency. *My* thoughts fell back upon themselves, unable to exit set recursive scenarios. A being moved and its *I* did not follow. To say I is to talk of a shell. Thawed out and transcendentally deprogrammed time held me as its own. Exiting the flat I was drawn to the negative expanse from which the flow of desire arose. I walked closer to those plugged in, those unconsciously communing with the flows of existence. I wanted my senses to be as close to the moment of acquisition as possible, to witness the very present in which a desire crossed the void into the real. I found that it came from precisely nowhere, an emptiness void of all anchoring; one could follow the trace of a single desire to the root of another stem and then follow that stem to a large root and on and on and on, before long one noticed they were cycling around and around in the very same spot, stuck within a system which vindicated itself *within* itself. It was deemed real because its prior parts had been deemed real.

It was not a *gate* for me then, but could be understood as one; this was the conundrum for many who troubled themselves with such ideas, what could be said of the impossibility of communication between the conditions and the reality developed from them, if such communication could be deemed true, then was it only unilateral or could we ever be able to venture to the other side. As I stood where and when I was the void was not a window nor a gate, nor anything, it was a whisper of phenomena, the most minor intuition of reality without any sense data ascribed to it; the closest one can get from the Inside to the Outside is by way of attunement to the processes of the stranger, the Other and the weird, for they all carry with them a trace of the Outside; it is felt as a gut-wrenching moment without cause, as if the closest of all companions has died, but whom also never existed, not an existential loss, but a loss concerning the meaning of loss altogether, a glimpse of a break in time itself...and then reality drags you back, *centers you,* puts you back into your territory, all warm and safe. At that moment, I had remained.

What can be said of the desires of the Other begs no length of thought, for either one shall find that we live in a collectively willed ignorance, in which we all avoid our black fate, or, one will find that they truly do exist amongst a collection of sleepy decaying apes. It was neither fleeting nor persistent, a moment of pure evaporation, it came about as quick as it wasn't, and before one knew it, there was a further intensity embedded in reality, drawing humans to and fro, altering relations and seemingly causing change; once the desire had emanated from nowhere, there was nothing which could commit it back to non-existence, it had become a possibility, a potentiality. This was why thoughts brought about the realities they willed, the emanations from the void vectored towards the head and hand could be considered the same. What is thought, of course, *becomes.*

Desire cannot be without a subjective formation of value, one which ascribes an abstract expense to *all* things. As such, there can be no such thing as a market if value and price are objectively absolute, if price followed value exactly there would be no marketization. Value becomes a subjective commodity that is reliant on a perpetual lack which increases and decreases in size concerning various subjectively contextual elements. One's lack becomes the project of fulfillment, the constant and endless drive towards further emptiness, for each desire-in-itself resides Outside of man's synthesis, and so to attend to that which one physically acquires as if that representation-in-itself held any answers is an ignorant task. One can spend their entire life attempting to fill a false lack with a false desire. They were not formed in such a way to say there was a hole within them, or gap, or physical lack; the lack was in connection to ongoing flux, perhaps there is little more tyrannous than an ever-flowing river amid a machine already begun.

In the midst of all connection, there was an infinity of empty happenings, moments targeted at an unattainable exterior, as fleeting in their fulfillment as they were in their arrival. What could be made of them was reliant precisely on what they left behind, a material to be poked and prodded, the skin of which had to be peeled off; a subject could keep peeling to the end of time and phenomena would never give. But what of the gate, where there is an entry there is an exit. As value and price did not match, neither did existence and objectivity, there was an impasse inherent within man's reality, the conditions for his language disallowed entry to the conditions themselves.

As any creation is the demise of its creator, any desire is the end of contentment. The moment the desire is born and the moment it is fulfilled are the same happening, acceptance of a chaotic spontaneity, to allow oneself over into the realm of irresponsibility, to admit the absurd into one's Being. For if there ever could be a completion, a filling of a cut or gape, a soft entry into the jagged dispersal of fleeting meaning, *if* there could be such a thing then no further words would be written. What is written and created continues to be so because of the very emptiness of a vacant existence; without filling one's time one is left with a duration solely awaiting the arrival of death, an admittance that there is no difference between being alive and being dead; desire draws the subject away from the point-blank synonymity of existence and non-existence.

The flows unto which all networked were, for man, the striated idolatry of becoming. To witness passionately writhing men, women and children be willingly dragged back and forth across this plane of intensity, little more than puppets gorging on the moments they hastily cut from the essence of existence. Beams of flames arising from nothingness, descending into hearts and minds, hands and cunts, bursting into chasms of intense momentary revelation; the moment-to-moment, second-to-second vectors of the herd were at once and always their most treasured past-times and lusts, the phantom of continuation had long ceased and what was left were remains of bitter children, scuttling between one trinket and the next, clawing at their latest God and forgetting about it in the same breath. The flows never ceased, jutting, expanding, contorting, collapsing, and ricocheting. But mostly one witnessed flows become stoppages, filing into areas and places, ideals, and singular understandings, emanating their worth into microcosms and dissipating into a veiled abyss.

The middle of a machine need not be thought of as a clunky array of parts, of wiring and circuitry. Nor does it need be thought of as some banal circulatory system, where there is blood and vitality, the territory of man is one where the middle of the machine is the middle of various temporal palpitations, fits of time and fevers of process, directions and haecceities arising as control mechanisms, latching to flesh and carrying it into bewildering ends. An indecipherable Outside leading those of language into a cacophony of noise and illusion, a rotting dog amongst a mound of treats, useless.

Slaves to time as slaves to process, never bereft of pleasure or pain, vice or virtue, always clinging to the warmth of an ideal, the coziness of the hampered and striated, *no-thing* is ever cast back and left alone, it all rolls into the tumult of confusion. Connected as fingernails embedded into a wound, clinging on not for dear life, but dear purpose, dear meaning, if one lets go of the object, they let get of the ego; to let go of desire was to let go of themselves and any anchoring their selves might have. Once they latched to a flow there was no going back, imagine, within all this, a float to keep hold of amongst the tides, an anchor as to say this is mine, and forever will be.

> *"Kant's object is thus the universal form of the relation to alterity; that which must of necessity be the same in the other in order for it appear to us. This universal form is that which is necessary for anything to be 'on offer' for experience, it is the 'exchange value' that first allows a thing to be marketed to the enlightenment mind"* [FN 67]

The whispers arose as inter-connected stimuli, diverging from the passage of a personal inner-sense and becoming nodes of luring conceptual intensification. Each auditory excitement of the Outside teased one to fragment further, to head deeper into the labyrinth and throw questioning to the wind.

My answers to difference and overcoming were to be found elsewhere. Everything I had come into contact with thus far had been something I had *already* known, something so completely absolute that it begged no further investigation in itself; I had to direct my thought towards the new in such a way that the unfamiliar arose. What use is a broom if you need to smash a window; the entire virtuality alters within the contextual and intellectual shift of the present. The materiality of phenomena is a fetishization for the same, one cannot desire that which they do not understand exists. The difference of the object cannot be found with the Other, unless one desires to get stuck in an-Other's dream, the difference is found by a manner of schizophrenic process. By a mode of understanding the abstractly beneficial traits of paranoia and neurosis one can begin to crack the ego wide open.

> *"difference as the wave or, more precisely, as 'the icy wave of eternity'"* [CG 44]

Difference has a pervasive existence, it is at once both real and unreal, real in its potential and unreal in its ability to appear of its own accord; the elusive in-between of difference and becoming was the point of communion, where one set aside stagnance and allowed themselves to be overcome by something other than *their* self. Something was prowling in from the Outside, like a weight on my thought, pressing it into corners and caressing it into rhythms of an artificial nature. Every thesis contains a kernel of its antithesis, the reaction, composition, and definition itself is reliant on the supposed external truly being internal; like a cancerous breakout and mutation, the internal inhumanity of man activates at the limitrophe of desire, when the object can no longer pull man further his *I* cuts itself to shreds and flounders schizophrenically at the edges of unification. The external is within, felt by all at moments of duress and solitude and silence, limit experiences need not be of so much grandeur and pomposity, one can wait for a few moments and the limit will always arrive, it is hospitality in relation to a limit which is one's grace. How does the herd react to limits but retreat as a collective, immediately birthing a repetition and folding themselves back into its arms and pace? To be stared at by flesh is to burn at the back, to light an all too human fire and react accordingly; to be stared at by the inhuman is to be momentarily awash with an icy coldness which freezes all functions in place, a gasp from a chasm of existence for but a second, and then, the human retrieves you with an inner-distraction - but what *is it* to *remain* in that empty-perturbation, that flow of duration without substance, the empty outside, the break in all vitality which ceases the rhythms of life...

Amidst all the flows and the guides and the connections, the locks and chains, whips and breaks, there could be said to be something called an 'ego', the most toxic lie of common reality. The ego, nothing but a fragile assemblage which falls apart at the meekest tap from the cosmos; the subjects hold it as *the* badge of existential honor, caressing and caring for it as we would a brain-dead infant, allowing it to be spoon-fed and cuddled, wrapped in blankets and wool. Nightly the ego has a seizure and revolts against its unification, awaking different but veiled as the same, one attempts to retrieve their past egos at the expense of their life.

One and all of these people could not hold onto their egos for they cannot hold onto time, one could say we are temporal amateurs, but truly we are reluctant acolytes of entropy. As the parts of selves fly in all directions and obliterate against boundaries, the clucking and nervous man is always left behind, tethered to an idea that changes so rapidly it is no idea at all; man wishes one thing where the ego is concerned, for all presents to adhere into a single blissful moment, a forever-childhood which makes sense to him and others, a clear-cut articulation of what a life should look like. But man cannot have this, it is not a possibility, the very nature of time outside of him makes it impossible for such an existence to ever be, and so, the ego is nothing more than a compilation of hypocrisy and absurdity. As the multitude of moments and events enter *in* they become paradoxical, and it is left to the apes to make sense of them. Presents handed over to tools specifically unable to investigate the reality they inhabit.

"Ever since it became theoretically evident that our precious personal identities were just brand-tags for trading crumbs of labour-power on the libidino-economic junk circuit, the vestiges of authorial theatricality have been wearing thinner." [ATA xiii]

It was all production and exchange. If I was to go by the voices then these interactions of man were just another market, the exchanges I saw were only a representation of something far greater and more malicious happening elsewhere, locked into definitions, no one can become that which they have been disallowed to become. There were alterations of color, style, clothing, shelter, taste, aesthetics, screens, data, work, entertainment, vices and virtues, but nothing different, never. Not at this level. How all this was maintained was simple, the internal-fascist clung to each piece of possession as tight as possible, for they believed it was not just something they owned, but something *of* them, and there is nothing we hold dearer than our own ideas about our self. Man clings to the external detritus of life in the belief that he is saving himself.

A woman before me was at one and the same time walking and laying on the floor. On the pavement she was naked, spontaneously vomiting a black acrylic substance against a brick wall. Tubes crammed into each orifice, her legs bound by hollow wire, toes spread and fingers pulled. Arms broken and held at disappearing angles. Her eyes burnt out and white. Hair growing rotten. Face with slight grin. Every time something entered all bonds got tighter and she became elated, letting out a minor epiphanic sigh, entering into a fever until the next flow; there were many alike this woman here, yearning, begging, crying out...weeping for anything to make entry, to fill them up, to block them; sometimes these people would look at one another in their states of closure and with moist eyes smile at their success of capture - Across the street, a mother broke all her child's limbs and tied it to a tree, hurling abuse at it, force-feeding it, they both agreed it was correct.

The street ballooned an organic defeat; sensation could not avoid the overthrow of flesh. My peripheral vision was filled with visions of intimate misery. Eye sockets hollowed out and scraped with a thick film of excrement, kneecaps punctured and stuffed with silver; ligaments pulled from biological hearth and wrapped around their masters. Jaws turned to paste under heel, skin peeled and rolled into mats. The voluntary action of an entire species was to walk into a thresher of degeneration and debasement ad infinitum. The resulting example of life a dribbling husk, obligated to its own subjugation. To ask why was fruitless, to question this mass of phenomenally masochistic ecstasy could only be but tyranny. I turned from the apes and their genitals, focusing on the process of dominion.

> *"The perceptual-consciousness system is a skin, lying 'on the borderline between outside and inside', (Beyond the Pleasure Principle) a filter, or a screen."* [FN 333]

It was instability itself, a soul flagellated on a paddle boat, the lake brazen with malice. Veils and gauzes between existences were not simple metaphors for the worried and concerned; what language attempted to articulate was a divide and what it *did* articulate, at all times, was its uncertainty and demoted nature, a lesser form of the Real, which sought not to *be,* but to describe; not to work, but to supervise; not to open up, but to wrap and contain; language could do nothing, and every note I took and every word I uttered and every thought I strained, each left a fidgety trace where language had been and language had tried, but nothing sticks to language which is why it takes so long to say anything at all. Nothing of beauty can be described, nothing sublime can be factored, nothing truly evil or good can be sampled; there is no faculty of man which permits him to share his experience, each and every notation is a failed gasp for any company at all. Documentation is implicitly scopophilic.

It was over for level 1 investigatory tactics, for anything the previous language attempted to grasp fell flat. A cosmic TV had been turned on for background noise, the noise being funneled into my being, slowly but surely the timber and softness of the voice arose, at times it felt fragmented, out of touch with itself, but other times it was very assured, as if it thought it truly belonged in my mind. There are always more questions: Where from? Why me? How does it enter? What is it made of? Is it real? And like most questions they end as quickly as they began, all that mattered, it seemed, over and over again, was how did I understand that which entered and how did *I* enter it as it had entered me, my exit was to be an entry back into that which I had left behind. Knowledge is a great paralysis, a death repeated; I know that there is more I will not know, and so to set forth is only an act of stepping ever backward.

So I didn't want to *know,* nor did I want to *accept* in the matter of an action; the voices happened and the time erupted, a subtle clatter in my mind, a rearranging of the furniture in my psyche and something else was now at home, I let it stay and sit, I allowed it to fester quickly; within what are known as minutes a madness of years can grow. Something is comforting in the arrival of desire, even as it appears from a dead nothing, even such a void can act as a beginning if one is ignorant enough. But what of voices that need duration and fostering, a style needs to be nurtured for it to find its feet; these voices were headless, fragmented morsels stripped of character, cold and vectored at the burn-core of existence. All organics began to systematize into a unification of parts and that which held them together trembled and weakened, the parts gripped one another in despair; for a body to beg that the soul let no more spirit in, before the dawn and realization that it is no spirit that beckons, but a skeleton-key-machinism, withering the spirit into a chronic pulp.

I went back to the flat. It no longer felt like a refuge. Temporally depleted and spatially fragile, I went to my bedroom in the misguided belief I may be able to sleep. I got into my bed for a while, existing solely within an artificially compiled atmosphere. No sounds or smells or sights arose naturally, each auditory experience rippled for too long, each smell intense or dull and each sight lagged upon its foundations. The flat was no longer held together by the empirical and the world had since forgotten it.

I had begun the process of pushing my-*self* to its utmost limits, I wished to become a stranger within my own body; allow my being to become entirely alien to its metaphysical reality. A possession via the forces of the Outside, a becoming-stranger, in which one becomes the physical embodiment and accepting vessel of Kantian genius; not that I am a genius in any rational sense, nor that I am genius at all, but that I was willing to *accept* genius to *use* me for a greater purpose; a channeling of the forces of various abyss', strewing them across the pithy assemblage I and others called I. Becoming-stranger, in the same vein as becoming-neurotic or becoming-paranoid, begins the process of detachment *away* from the human-security-system, that cursed articulation of all that I was, and would ever be stuck within, and made *of.* This was a process of immanentization, an alteration of material reality from the Outside in; a paradox which would once have caused me great discomfort now only blocked off such comforts by becoming my only reality, I was entering into space where feeling and emotion could not *be,* nor *become.*

> *"That which is strange is not a passive object of revulsion, but a dynamic principle of departure and migration."* [CG 93]

The voice marked its own duration, all reflection stopped as it commenced its didactic invasions. Unable to fully let his-self erode, man builds kingdoms which leads him to believe control is on his side, the development of an aesthetic as a way to signify freedom. Freedom does not belong to the empire of signs, it is found within the process of recognizing animality; as one bows to the shoreline and takes their leave, the only exit is to be washed *Out,* into the boundless oceanic abyss.

Quite literally unable to sleep I walked back into the center of town. There was no one around anymore, not a soul or personality to be found or gawped at. Lights still hummed in odd rhythms, and the tarmac pulsed slightly. I couldn't feel nauseous, but I wanted to. The spirit of the town had vanished, even the most banal brand atmospheres had faded, and everything had become a shop front, a set of the drabbest design, a balsa-wood existence. Entry to any of the buildings was instinctively forbidden; I understood that the further lack of conclusion might cause unneeded panic. Bereft of source even the taste in my mouth had been discontinued, my senses had been culled to their kernel, no longer interpreting, only *allowing.* I returned to the flat and got into my car which was parked around the back. Surprisingly, the engine started quicker than usual, the gears were smoother too, almost frictionless. I headed towards the nearest city. As I exited the town there was no transition, I was within a space which was then within another, there was no more to it than that; movement had become inconsequential.

The usual route beckoned me *not* to take it, but I pushed through that wall of intuition and continued down a habit. The road continued for far longer than usual, bending in on itself without a curve. It kept going and no potential movement accompanied me. I drove for hours down the same road, the scenery altering only in vague repetitions like the background of an old cartoon, eventually patterns always emerge. I slowed the car so my eyes could adjust to this backdrop. It was dulled out, placid, and flat. I stopped the car and stood alongside the road, looking not into but *at* the horizon, it was as if I could reach out and grab it, tear it. It was a prop before my face, useless and floating. I got back into my car and checked the petrol gauge. I had driven 333 miles away from the town. I hesitated before checking my rearview mirror, it wasn't working, it showed only my face looking forward. I exited the car as it no longer stood for its known use, and so I sensed nothing when experiencing it now. I feared what lay on the path back. I turned. Before me, 333 miles out of town, was the town. I had traveled and not traveled, such an event in time leaves one only to the whims of that which wishes you to do or not do X or Y. Any removal from these rails was an exercise in futility, and I didn't wish for that fatigue. The atmosphere grinned at me, the cosmos was being misanthropically coy. I drove back into town; this took no time at all. I parked up and sat on a bench in the center of the marketplace, it drew me to it. I sat for weeks and minutes thinking about what I might do, all thought stopped at the point of choice regarding action. I looked up and upon the corner of a building which concealed a path leading to the seafront. But I understood that I was to wait a while longer, I didn't want to disturb any workings here; any potential disturbance would have been worked out anyway. I was an intrigued slave, caressing his chains with a hidden delight.

A figure appeared at the corner roughly 100 meters away, but that metric was useless now. The figure stood in plain sight looking directly at my location. We looked at one another for a while, I could discern no image. I finally panicked, I was no longer bound with life; I didn't want my mother or a teddy bear, nor did I wish to leave. The figure's presence was neutral, that of a tour-guide. And at that thought the figure slowly turned and headed towards the seafront, my inner sense was lost and all that would happen was already there waiting for me, I had only to remove, shed and admit for the path to fully open. I followed the figure at a distance; space can offer little security once one's anxiety is targeted at reality itself. We made it to the seafront, it was too empty and had no wind, the sand bereft of nostalgia and its past a hazy lie. The ocean stood as it always did, with the allure of chaos and calm, perturbating to the rhythms of its own existence, a pulsing circuitry which found truth only in its flows. A little way out to sea was a boat, I hadn't noticed it before, now it was all I could see. It was an old cargo ship, a fishing vessel with tires strung around the outside, it held no name. On the shore the figure lurked by a small rowing boat, waiting for what must come next. It began to prepare the boat as I began walking towards it. I was quickly sat in it and being rowed to the nameless ship. The figure looked over me, past me, onto me, into me, through me and around the sky, but all hope of catching sensible contact was thwarted by my cognition, I cannot tell you what that figure looked like, what constituted its face never settled for me, and beyond that my mind was disallowed interest. What was of merit to me, even in that landscape, was that there was no hostility to be found with the figure, not to say there was no active danger or risk, but there was certainly no malicious intent, only rigorous investigation. The figure rowed and I did not, and that's how it was at that moment.

I was rowed out to the Nameless Ship by the figure, we didn't speak. There was no content to speak of, only the grasping at a previous life, one which I knew had no bearing, meaning or purpose to it, and to bring it up would be only to admit to the desire for comfort, and no such desire will ever bring about its object. Up until now, the past had been a series of seemingly interlocking events, none of which had merited much attention. Every socially pressured achievement had fallen flat at the moment of completion. I finally gained enough gall to speak about the situation at hand, terrified of course, that doing so would make it real; it's always tough to talk coherently in dreams, and so I was already testing this reality which my pronouncement-

"Traditionally, shouldn't we be on a river...if this is *that* kind of journey?"

> *'Reason in its legitimate function is a defence against the sea,'* [ATA 107]

I wasn't sure if the figure had spoken from its body, or only to my thoughts, did it matter, the sentence was clear, not a schizophrenic whisper from behind the ear, but a clear cryptic-comment channeling pseudo-comforting humanity. The accent in my mind was reminiscent of Old England, quiet and subtle, largely comforting yet not warm. There was a tonal inflection at the end as if to imply there was more, always more. But I couldn't argue, I had no faculty, my jaw and throat felt like dry pulp, and there was little to say anyway. What of the comment itself though? I had made the quip about the river to ease my alienation; the journey into madness along the linearity of the river, a classic. Perhaps the linearity here was important, for if what it said of rivers is true, then what one can say of the sea is merely devoid of implicit structure, you can go mad in *all* directions here. I yearned for a river, those comforting banks on either side, the ability to quickly ground one's self if you so wish; but the ocean, the sea, that great selfish calamity, roaring in all its beauty, it is pure possession, the deeper you venture, the more currents you begin to interact with; madness opens further passages to even greater madness. I had to release any desire to see land, I wanted no territory.

Reason, not exactly the riverbank itself, but it was most definitely that oh-so-human system of security, reason is the creation of riverbanks where there are none, a means to ground oneself in a multiplicity of torrents. It defended man against the idea he wasn't in control. The sea soon teaches man he is not in control; at least nowhere near as much as he liked to think. It was of no surprise to me that the Greek for cybernetics comes from *Kubernetes*, meaning steersman. Upon entering the sea one is approaching a question of control and mastery, to where and when will one be pulled. Within the ocean the subject becomes fragmentary, dispersed upon a multitude of non-linear pathways; madness is oceanic.

The Nameless Ship

The figure boarded the ship first. It didn't lend me a hand, only retreated to the main deck. I boarded shortly after, climbing an old rope ladder and setting foot on the decaying flooring. From the shore, the ship seemed complete, but now it was at hand it seemed fragmented, a collection of eras compounded into a disheveled bundle, a relic of times entirely displaced. I understood that I was not to head inside just yet and so I sat at the rear of the ship, on a wooden shelf that was jutting out. I lit a cigarette and thought about my situation. The nicotine altered my state in no discernable way. I looked to the shore, the tide had no rhythm, jerking and glitching against the sand in bursts, some sections remained whilst others retreated, it had been evicted from its rhythmic home. The horizon above the shore withdrew inwards, folding into a dot which both quickly and cosmically slowly disappeared. There was no longer anything for me to be washed upon, or to look towards, what now? Now that nihilism is of no comfort? I was at the whim of the vessel which held to the sea as life holds to the universe, in the most fragile of vibrations; I felt what it was to fluctuate at the limitrophe of existence, an impatient swipe away from pure nothingness.

I finally stood, intent on heading towards the ship's small bridge, hoping to introduce myself to our captain. The floor was littered with crab buckets, strewn paper, and rotting wood. I opened the cabin door to find not only no captain but no means of steering the ship. The inside of the cabin was uncannily smooth as if the textures hadn't loaded in, as if this area was simply not for me. I should have felt nauseous, but without progression, I had only the idea of vomiting to comfort me. I understood once again, a layered understanding, further hopelessness; there was nothing for me to do. The vessel understood too, and so the Nameless Ship began its journey. I looked overboard, the sea seemed further away than the bottom of the boat, the splash and spray out of sync with our movements. We were using the sea, not assimilating into it. All I could do was trust its communication. It moved in absurd lines and flows, odd trajectories mimicking a broken piece of graphics, *with* its surroundings, but not *of* them.

The hatch to the inside was now open and I had little else to do but go in. I waited a while before my descent inside, holding patiently against the oceanic mirage. The sea was everything and nothing all at once, a meek discord of potential, captured and set-free, it was irrational at heart. The helmsman is led by the odor of history, the stench of form and meaning; the irreducible guff of linearity is but a lure for those of weak temperament, what to say of the anonymous helmsman? The dead helmsman? A route is something caught up within representation, likewise, a path and vision amount to the sameness of any end. Once the cause is signified the battle is already over, and neither side knows the victor, for it has already fled into the embrace of the virtual. The figure briefly looked up from inside the ship, up to where I was standing and gawping at the empty wheelhouse. One who leads, the idea that there is one *in charge,* that there could be some direction, even if it's into a burning fire, is this not where we find any comfort? Every facet of controlled duration is held together by an approximate presumed vector, we always have to be *going* or *doing* or *heading;* the death drive was never some compulsion for obliteration, but a meta-comfort-blanket, the urpath of one's life. One might be heading into a slow, drawn-out, atomically abysmal death of rot and mulch, but at least that's a *direction!* I descended into the ship.

The inside of the ship was almost entirely books, except for a few random jars of assorted fungi and seaweed, a crib which was without a mattress, and two hardback wooden chairs, one occupied by the figure. Upon closer inspection, the books were primarily on Qabbalah, Gematria, and mathematics. I turned to the figure. It was staring directly out to sea via a small porthole. It had been a long time since I'd felt such heart-throbbing despair, Cioran and Ligotti get you close, but they're both men, and so are always thwarted in their attempts to convey what the universe does oh-so naturally. I sat in the other chair, across from the figure. I lit another cigarette and placed my head in my hands. In movies people often scream at times like these or at least seize up, that's not the reality. Screaming, much like worrying, never helped any situation, complacency takes over; Sisyphus was happy at first, then mad, then inquisitive, then silent, then fatigued and finally, submissive.

> *'Despair can get things started, if it means the abandonment of diverting idols'* [XS *Dark Moments*]

The figure's voice once again rang silently clear. What use is it to fight against one's will, deep down there are many who yearn for madness, for sanity has offered them no resolve. I wish, truly, that I hadn't been one of those people, but alas, I was, and so all there was left to do was to give into the voices. And what of idols, I had none. I was brought up within a Church of England school, and so it was practically mandatory that I become an atheist. The only time I covertly-prayed was when I wanted something, and I hadn't desired anything in a long time. I had little to nothing to abandon in theory, the practice of abandonment, however, is far more harrowing, there's always more to be given up than one first suspects.

I thought of old friends and family, the life I could have chosen, and yet those questions of what one could do if they *could* change the past are all false wishes, pleading to the universe for some hint at meaning. You only become *from* all the paths you take, and so going backward is only ever a repetition back into the present. I beg of erasure from the only position I can, the one in which I have already learned what I desire to be erased.

I attempted to fixate on something...anything, an anchor of duration which I believed may allow me some temporal positioning or territory. As if in a spontaneous tease a seething red buoy floated by upon the horizon, I peered out of the porthole, my gaze held steadfast to this comforting territory. Nothing in me could keep up or ever approach the buoy; it was at all times, in all times. Each iteration which passed my filter became its own microcosm of dead temporality, detached of connectedness and purpose, duration skipped maliciously on all horizons, and I did no more than sit and become decentered within myself.

> *"Time produces itself in a circuit, passing through the virtual interruption of what is to come, in order that the future which arrives is already infected, populated."* [FN 358]

The whisper was glib, touching on temporal paradox as commonplace. The figure appeared as a stack of simulations, all overlapping and unfocused. It reclined into the chair as other shadows prodded at the pages of various texts, no single outline ever becoming truly defined.

I walked out onto the deck of the ship, sitting on the surrounding railing and immediately entering a trance of no particular focus; one becomes transfixed in the very act of duration itself and phenomena fades into passivity. The flows of waves evaporated against the immediacy of invisible barriers; the wind soared at definitive angles. As I remained still a sense of potentiality welled up inside the atmosphere, and as I breathed it jolted into an arrhythmia. Nothing could keep up with itself, nor will it ever be able to; one need wish that time never identically attends to itself, in that moment everything is lost and something else altogether has won.

I sat atop the boat for some time, admiring and falling into what the world was giving me, unable to retain its past nor anticipate its future, a present-death, time and time again. A temporal nomad washed into the shores of time-itself. Occasionally I would check my pulse, it made no sense to me, there was an implicit disconnect, organic rhythms were elsewhere. All the boats creaks and bows were delayed, everything was both in an act of catching-up and rushing ahead, to get sight of some object was immediately to lose it.

At distinct times the wind would pass on by, latching to the curls of my shoulders and back, a caress fluttering into a void; bereft of retention all ancient forms ceased, dead gales unable to carry the weight of myth, beholden only to the Outside, working perpetually at the limit. To say the time carried my humanity away would be incorrect, humanity is falsely caught up in time, and it has a false hegemony over that which only tortures it. There was no space here, only moments created by and for time, temporal-places from which things can be toyed with. There can be no torture without duration; the space of the sadist is inconsequential, it is how he teases one with time which is of importance. The patient executioner, the belated flogging, a scalping deriving its beauty from spiraling off into the eternal, what joyous ecstasy...

I got up from where I was sitting, adjusting to the turbulence of real-time. To give temporality any possibility of curvature is to open pathways to God's corpse; I thought of the men of my old town, awaiting the arrival of a meaningful nothing, a guiding trademarked star to position their present from; an arrival makes the reality implicit before the phenomenal fact, any flows that *arrive* have already been on their way.

The distinct problem with the helmsman is that however experienced he or it is, there is always that which he will have to succumb to, admit to, or accept. Forces out of *his* control. It is not the task of a good helmsman to sail his course, but only to navigate what fate hands him with great skill. I turned my attention back to the sea, I thought of Serres sat upon a French sailing ship, somber and quiet; what can one say of a fate disjointed in time? Fate itself is a transcendental error perpetuated due to its implicit comfort regarding failure, pain, and betrayal. I could not think of a helmsman-out-of-time;

was it a shipwreck which had overcome its definition. The sea grinned with every crash of waves. At least a ship within a flowing sea acts as a contract, a point where a possible continuum might develop, what of a sea within stagnant, dead time. Nothing for a helmsman to work with; existence preceding essence is a freedom, an essence denied its existence is lifelong torture. The Nameless Ship was a free-floating vessel adrift in a dead and useless time; an object as a carrier, a toy for time to play around with, and, as it *always* does, get bored with.

If I was to look anywhere for a great helmsman, it seemed to be precisely nowhere. I stood against the railing, looking down upon the old tire fenders, they held absolutely, stuck somewhere alien to me. Wherever I looked caused a rupture of understanding, I retreated to the pleasures of sound, its reassuring timbre, refrain, and smoothness. It ceased. Even turning my neck became a silent undertaking, the internal noises of the body had fallen away, the world was caped in a cold silence, of which nothing could pierce. Silence is the only reality; amidst conversation, a halting silence can turn one's stomach inside out and destroy civilizations; language erodes against the abrupt cliff of silence.

> *"From the perspective of doom — only glimpsed, slowly, after vast disciplines of coldness — everything you are trying to do is a desperate idiocy that will fail, because humanism (hubris) is the one thing you can never let go."* [XS *Doom Circuitry*]

I had relaxed into the voice and I no longer froze as it spoke. At first, I pushed myself to exhaustion to truly *listen* to what I was being told, putting a quasi-conscious effort into my replies. At last, I became lucid, allowing the concepts to echo from the Outside In.

Language becomes an afterthought, a humanist shell keeping everything safe and coated in flesh; the signifier and *to* signify, there could not be any easier way of stating that one wishes to be kept warm by the same. What's on the 'other side' of the human can yet to be said to be anything at all, frontiers are inherently paradoxes - if one understands what it is to succeed a limit, the limit has already been succeeded. We *crave* that which will finally define us, which in turn will be that which will destroy us. *Anything,* whose substance can allow the compounded ignorance, narcissism, and resentment made-flesh that is a *man* to be defined, shall surely, as its first principle, obliterate the great plebeian apes of Earth. Most people don't get close to despair at all, before one can truly despair there must be a season of humanistic depressions and anxieties, and each must be cast off and understood as what it truly is, an indulgent act; man's agony, alas-alas, one sits and despairs, oh poor man - this is not despair, this is the romantic virtue built by the whiniest of grifters; the poets, the lovers, the sops and hearts, they get no closer to despair than they do anything of beauty. The peak of a summit which only looks back down upon the path tread by man, family, or country can be said to be nothing more than a psychotherapeutic paddy.

I thought often of my thoughts and the process of thinking, what it was to think *here,* what might be happening to my understanding. Painfully slowly and yet all at once, I realized that such thoughts were entering into a recursive loop of admittance and allowance. There was only going to be so much that I would be allowed and any alterations which were deemed outside of this experience would be false, illusions of my creation; an aesthetic of difference can carry you very far, but only if you allow the ego more rights than it ever deserved, rights which will eventually consume it altogether.

> *"To be a carrier is to be pushed beyond the limits of human possibility, to explore those regions where only an inorganic and artificial thinking is able to plot itself. Carriers know only what they need to know and no more."* [XS *Hyperstitial Carriers III*]

What is it that advances man? An oversocialization of his creation, man wishes to fornicate with the monster. All I could ever write down was what I would be allowed to write down, any attempt to push within a push is already thwarted, you cannot accelerate acceleration, if you could it would have already folded the anticipation of the limit back into itself. One is not the catalyst, but a mere pawn of communion awash with symptoms of anthro-existence. Optimism, pessimism, cynicism, nihilism - these all crumple into themselves at the first inability to acknowledge the real; nor can they ever attend to their most certain fate of being prefixed with neo or hyper, a hyper-nihilist is the stacking of a non-statement, a multiplication of 0.

Everything organically human falls away at abstract limits, vitality gets sucked into a thresher of production, the incandescence of the soul homogenizes and the breath of life is lost.

Anything human had to be stripped away like a symptom of something far greater than any *self* could be. Like the rot of the collective in miniature, every human yearns for emancipation from the possibility of connection to the great torso, the clumsy lump of flesh which mimics a guide.

> *"Acephalization = schizophrenia."* [FN 397]

Ah, but the head to be without flesh turns into something else altogether, a shambling schizo-bum, tripping up on the rug of Oedipus, alien to it, hostile to its omnipotence. It's only time which allows growth, and thus I am beholden to Chronos for the possibility of warmth or love; when they arrive in an instant, the oh-so-human vitalism of the heart is to be distrusted. What could come then of a dead-sea, a current without time as men understood it; each love, of mutt or woman, faded into inconsequentiality, a diamond marriage dissipating into ashes. To wake on a spring day they say, as if that has any meaning at all. I'll tell you what spring is, it's an abject temporal monstrosity, burgeoning at the seams with arrogant ethereality and patronizing glory; give me late autumn, give me the nights of winter, but oh dear lord, allow me the mercy of spring, with its false hope and aesthetic rebirth.

Each heartfelt moment a pulsation of faith in the beat that has eternally betrayed its owner. I loved and breathed and fucked and yearned and wanted and needed and desired...and what of them, as quickly as they were sought, they were washed to the past and the present became lost once again; the ambivalence of pleasure over pain, the apathy of that which makes man himself is so fickle; a quasi-conscious glob of decaying flesh, awash between two eternal shores, clutching onto a language-blanket, perpetually muttering empty words to make it grow, to keep himself afloat against the ever-present nothing.

But when to let go, and what is it to let go; to watch language and all moorings float away and disappear from vision as soon as your clutch loosens, this is what it means to decapitate oneself and let the remains be overtaken by the atemporality of the Outside. A headless torso, streaming blood into the circuitry of oceans, enthusing with the waters of the inhuman and alien, a merging, cross-contamination, the mass of the schizophrenic is a sacrifice to nothingness itself, to give all possibility and potentiality of self over to something not greater than one, nor lesser, but over to a chasm of bellowing laughter, possession by the unknowable, incalculable and uncorrelatable.

The flows of the sea surrounding the boat were nauseating, not in their actual tampering with the movement of the boat, but their cadence. Waves collided at right angles and the geometry of all circuitry fell from its bed of causal springs. A multitude of rivers coalescing into abstract chaos; there was not a single wave I could latch my sight onto just before it buzzed into an unrecognizable pattern. At first, there seemed to be no relationships here, no networks or structures, but then I gathered that as you don't plug a PC into the internet directly, you need a router to process the data; I had been inserted into the Other without due preparation, without relation or comparison, all connection voided and assimilation made mandatory. At least one can relate to their captor or master in the manner of a victim or slave; what of a non-master, who isn't even aware of the subject's predicament, let alone cares of it.

> *"Look what it did to Kurtz, a special forces ultra-capital meat-machine hacked and cored-out by K-virus, touched by a dark future, recycled through hell."* [FN 409]

The whispers became more abstract and malicious, complete with a tendency to teach whilst simultaneously destroy, as if the processes were synonymous. The process and potential patterns became clearer, convergency was their primary objective, and any convergent future was dark for the mere fact of its pull. The time of this ocean was a grand-matter of convergence and divergence, both folded into a greater convergence; if the fragmentation and dispersion of nature didn't leave the remainder with purpose, with an enduring towards a point or newness, then anthropocentric notions of nature were pointless too. The ocean pooled as it fluctuated sporadically, the surface was a mess, the top of the waves a screaming and flamboyance of assumed control, each splash wishing to retain its reality as that of the utmost importance; as one gazed deeper absolutely nothing stared back, that would be a truly optimistic idea, that something down *there* cared about whether you saw it or not. All a subject can see when they stare into an oceanic depth is a reflection, and the conclusions you draw from such a mirror are beholden to a humanist narcissism. 'Oh, lo-and-behold the great crashing sea!' shrieks the self-infatuated, 'Oh mighty sea, oh deep waters, the great deep, forgiveth one thy sins!' and on and on, as if such concentration were of merit.

There was *that* which *was* there though, it was not a forlorn abyss or a hellish burn, nor was it epiphanic or enlightening, what resided at the depths of all oceans was the inability of all correlation. There was nothing there *to* stare back, and if an abject nothingness is the conclusion of horror, then I would state the subject is stuck within itself. I wasn't *there* yet, an attempt was underway to get me close. It's said '*They will be made to crawl on their bellies into the Kingdom of darkness*', I was sliding on my gut, bloated and bored, the boat carried me further than any anthro-flatulence could, I owed my passage to an anonymous helmsman, as soon as identity is in the mix, any truth is lost.

It continued as it had to. Sometimes it was day, sometimes it was night, and it was always slightly cool. The last few minutes and years and seconds and aeons of the journey came hurtling in, as one arises from a blackout, all-at-once pulled into another consciousness, with no recollection - except in memory and concept - of the night before; haunts algorithmically arose and clutched to the next, my thoughts a succession of maybes and not-possibles. We'd arrived at a point, at a distinction, at a collapse in continuity.

The ship pulled to a halt, bridging two realities. Doing so in such a way that as one turned their sensibility from one to the other, there was nothing to suggest the proximity of the other as being so close and potentially intrusive. I had been sat with the figure for *some* time, a length, a succession, it needn't have mattered, my brain couldn't keep it in. The figure's quarters had remained intact, not one jot of dirt seemed to have moved or swayed, a pure-lifelessness emanated from everything down there. I got up from the hard-backed chair, made an attempt at a refreshing stretch, learning nothing, and understood I must get on deck, though I had no recollection of returning to the ship's quarters. And so I did, moving routinely to the hatch, opening it, and setting foot once more Outside.

The ship was still. I walked to the bow and gazed around. Before me was the sea, at a dead stop, not a single ripple, with its depths ending abruptly before descending into any dark hue. There was an emptiness of the sensible for this horizon, an expanse which time had since left and forgotten, potentially to be used once more, or left forever, it was not for me to say. The back-end of time held blueprints of forgotten digressions, ignored potential, unproductive realities...all left somewhere, existing in the absence of will, beyond the frontier of all intelligible care. The more I held myself towards this horizon, the more my thoughts faded into inconsequential rationality.

As I turned there was a moment, a point, and everything changed. An apprehension without need for the legitimacy of continuity; what followed the drag of my senses was complete virtuality, which arrived prepared. I halted my sight, breathing faint and limbs empty yet heavy. The city within my view was that of Königsberg. It was rotting, the distant brickwork disheveled, the sky a deep gasp from a dying lung. The dock was far above the city, yet immanent to its mapping. The entire world trembled momentarily before being pulled back in a manner of repression, the city was weak, it was being held together; the skyline procedurally generated with my senses, the wind entering into repeated routines, various pangs and twinges were plotting throughout my body. As I held to the railing of the ship, I looked to the dock, at once it was at my feet. I turned back to find my hands still clasped to the rail, my senses caught between desires, wills, and Others, and yet, the theatre of it all acted as a unification; I was being teased for not entirely submitting. There is an exhaustion that needs to come with complete submission, one needs not just all energy to have dissipated, but all hope, and all hope of hope; for a man to truly submit to the forces of the Outside he need give up everything that makes him man, and there are few who even come close to the limit, let alone the practice.

Königsberg

I began to think of *The Critique of Pure Reason,* going through the basics in my mind, attempting to trigger something from the figure who now stood before me. No amount of prying my mind did anything, perhaps I was too wrapped up in my own biases, only a lacuna can trigger cosmic-interjection, Cunningham's law worked only for a human needing to prove their status, the universe already had its proofs. The figure eventually headed towards the ship's ladder, calculating a slow glance towards me as it did so. As I looked at the top of the ladder I noticed that it dropped directly onto a street, whilst the rest of the ship still sat upon the sea. I supposed once time is playing around as it wants to, space is little more than an afterthought.

I descended the ladder and stepped out onto the street, immediately looking towards an antique two-story house, entirely symmetrical with three windows on either side of the front door. I took a couple of steps forwards and turned to look back at the ship, it was in front of me in the sea, and however slowly I turned my head back towards the house, the transition between the two realities was both seamless and timeless, there was no moment of connection, only either one of forgetting or incompatibility.

> *'there cannot, according to the Kantian construction, ever be a secret about space as such. Space understood transcendentally as a pure form of objective intuition, rather than as an object cannot contribute to the content of a private experience.'* [CC 1.13]

The figure had been watching me turn my head and so it spoke to me, this was *my* guess. It was the second time the figure had referenced Kant, though not even directly, only concerning his content as a thinker as if Kant was a pawn in a great system where biography was merely a symptom for those who forever needed training wheels.

Despite the endless sea and its failure to accord to any strict pattern of turbulence, I had grown fond of the Nameless Ship, a fondness which was not reciprocated. As I stared back at the vessel, there was no thought of the reality behind me being possible, let alone being *there,* and yet everything about the boat and the sea, at that moment, was solid. Not like a rock or mountain, both of which are beholden to the tortures of time, but solid with respect to a forbidden eternity, one which would never falter or shake until certain events had been played out. There was a cryptic meaning - I assumed - in the events taking place and the whispers in my mind, which thus far had come from a single voice, that of the figure. I thought on the spaces I was between, void of connection in their representation, but connected by a hidden link, time. The master and possibility of all, the maleficent controller, parasitically dominating each level via different methods, causing all alteration and cause; always, in thought, a return to something deeper and irretrievable; pinned to a wall and allowed to gaze *across* a frontier, but never permitted to set foot beyond its horizon.

I turned back to the city, attempting to forget the boat, attempting to submit myself to the atmosphere which begged me to accept things as they were, the boat was over, it was temporally *done,* even if some banal *space* remained. I looked at the city, it was abstractly composed as a lazy cartoon, aesthetically real, and yet in places vitally dead. Distinct paths, patterns, and areas lured one by the promotion of their palpable difference, all else a cardboard reality, flimsy and unearned.

Eventually we stepped away from the ship and into the front garden of the house. It was simultaneously overgrown and neatly cut, the blades of grass altering diagonally in the fragmented wind. We stopped just before the front gate, looking upon the house itself, it seemed to hold two existences, the rot beckoning through, before the idealism returned atop its vibrations. The front door began to slowly open. I understood it was 3:33 pm, but that thought quickly evaporated into an absence of meaning.

Out of the front door stepped the man himself, Immanuel Kant. As he moved through the front garden I realized all was amiss, unusual, and uncanny. His movements were clunky as if his reality couldn't keep up with some simulation veiled over his body. He was having trouble keeping in sync with the Real. As he got closer I felt uneasy, I had always wanted to ask him many questions, I prepared myself, but as he grew nearer I understood that questions were not an option. He briefly halted at the garden gate, his head turning stiffly towards me and the figure, looking directly through us. His jaw had become unhinged, there was a metal plate glistening in the false sunlight. *"I have traced a path which I will follow. When my advance begins, nothing will be able to stop it. "* he stated clinically. His head returned to a front-facing position. He began moving towards the city, I attempted to call after him, catching him up and placing my hand on his shoulder, he didn't flinch, let alone recognize any difference in the act.

We continued a few meters before I finally looked down, his coat-tails covered no feet, where once were boots now stood a metal beam, sunk deep into the road. Kant was on rails! From what I could work out this system was old, it had a dated aesthetic which reminded me of theme park animatronics. I and the figure followed him for some time, just before reaching the town center he turned back to look at us, his metallic jaw now melting his synthetic skin, *"Land, Land, my dear friends, I see Land."*, I recognized the quote from De Quincey's *The Last Days of Immanuel Kant*, now it was some sick joke.

We continued following Kant into the heart of Königsberg. The city folk all moved and contorted mechanically in rhythm with Kant's no longer existing steps. The 'Königsberg Clock' was not his nickname, it was his reality, he was the chronic temporal master of this city. The city moved in time with Kantian mechanics, the whole place was an amusing torture of temporal aesthetics. Women came to their windows and waved to Kant during his walk, many of them shells of their past animatronic-selves, metallic limbs and wiring going haywire. A little way ahead of us Kant halted, we caught up to him to find that the wind had caused his fraying jacket to come away at the seams, beneath his lapels was a dated, rotten chassis.

We arrived at the market square, everywhere I looked I witnessed the backend of the Inside, the people of Königsberg had been cruelly locked to a system capturing them within a minute reality, disallowing anything other than the immediate presentation at hand. Kant seemed to have immanentized himself into this reality as a final touch, the master subsumed into his creation. Every door, every window, every organ, and breath was hardwired into a mass of circuitry, it seemed as if it all flowed back to Kant, but as I tried to follow it I quickly got lost, it started and ended in multiple places, I could find no end or beginning, and when I did, they quickly disappeared and became other things entirely. I stood before Kant pondering the situation, the prison-at-hand. There was Being behind the automatism, a pulling against the rails, but a distinct apathy towards their inability to escape. Many of them looked at their feet as they walked, watching as the rail beneath them guided their movements; transcendental puppets given the clearest vision of their fate.

> *"The perceptional consciousness system is a skin, lying 'on the borderline between outside and inside', a filter, or a screen."* [FN 333]

The figure stood the other side of Kant, admiring his circuitry. Its statement pertained to our entire perception, the problem of Königsberg, the barrier between the common reality of the Inside and the elusive Outside. The Outside isn't that which is not part of some circuitry, neither real nor metaphorical circuitry such as institutions or authority, the Outside is pure-time, it is that which is before anything else, before all syntheses take place by man – or anything else for that matter. I continued to stare at the tyrannous rails, what use was it to know that they were there? How did that help anything? My anthropocentric view was interrupted –

> *"Boxes not only have a shape, but also an inside & an outside, which means – at least implicitly – a transcendental structure. They model worlds and suggest ways out of them."* [XS *Pandora's Box*]

The figure gestured to the rail beneath my feet as it stated its claim. There I was on the burgeoning temporal island of Königsberg, being locked in by a mechanical tendril.

> "*This is why in Deleuzian critique syntheses are considered to be not merely immanent in their operation, but also immanently constituted, or auto-productive.*" [FN 321]

The figure made it clear, it didn't matter if the tendril locked on, if there has even been one such mechanism then transcendental temporality has begun, caught like a fly in burning ember, between two elusive sides of a non-linear auto-catalytic labyrinth. The mechanism of the transcendental, its circuitry, produced itself.

I thought back to all those books on Kant, all those forum posts and conferences, hastily trying to construct an answer to this riddle. Kant was always the point of no return with regards to philosophy, which is to say, the bleeding-edge of reality. If one took Kant's conclusions - *all* to be found, in some form, within the first critique - seriously, then nothing else in life mattered...for a time. Time & space are *a priori,* that is, they *are* before any experience, you don't need to experience them to know them, because *they are needed* for there to be any *possibility* of experience altogether. As I thought, the figure patiently assessed my thought process. Time is of course prior to space, for space has to be *in* time. From this I drew the following conclusions:

Man must exist *in* time and space, and yet, man is a miserably unique case regarding both. Firstly because we can self-analyze, we can, as *I* was, attend to our predicament of existence. But secondly and most importantly, we, us, humans, attend to time and space...reality, via *our* senses, which are *processed* by our brains, and so how man perceives matter is entirely synthetic, we do not *sense pure* time and space as they actually are, but only as *re-*presentations...representations of that true reality, that Real. Our reality is created as we - our organs of perception - represent it, everything we sense is quite simply, not really what it is, it's not the Real. Well, even *if* what we perceive was in fact the Real, we could never say it was, the epistemological structure at hand is not one in favor of man, and as such, we're always in a bind of unknowing, the Real haunts our every sensible moment. Space is secondary to time, which according to Kant is what our inner sense processes to formulate its outcomes. Time is that which we structure our reality *from.* All secrets are hidden not in space, but in time; a secret hidden in space is only the phenomenological idealization of a secret, a pithy lie; all pure secrets are folded into time. What can the inner sense of man be then other than a cage? The 'external' time of the Outside - prior to being synthesized by man on the Inside - is not the time *we* experience, we are locked in, but locked into what exactly? All of this is torture, I am thinking through the details of the black iron bars whilst they mock me. A chronic, linear, suffocating, and distinct form of temporal progression, constructed as a falsity of phenomena.

And now what of all that determinist, free will debate? What can be said of these classical arguments after Kant...very little, if anything at all? The past, the present, and the future, these are not times, but errors in anthropocentric optimism.

'*You cannot have time in time.*' [Hermitix Interview]

The figure condensed my thoughts. Our time is a false layer, the ticking of the clocks is a lie, hours and minutes are only a meaningful metric if you believe them to be, what happens when you allow all succession to cease its illusions - a second is the same as any other, a moment of nothingness, an application of pure subjectivity constraining your existence to a detectable rhythm, what are production and consumption without the swing of the pendulum, mere unquantifiable phenomenal actions. Our time is a representation of time *in* time and as such is not time itself, so...*when* the hell am I? Space doesn't matter anymore, the anymore it used to exist in - as a coherence - has been dissolved by these temporal theatrics. To venture into *pure* time, what then?

"*To undertake such a task is to follow Trakl into cobwebbed vaults that few have wished to enter.*" [CG 133]

I had to disagree with the figure here regarding the supposed *wish* to enter such vaults. One can say of entry that it is no mere wish or desire, but a calling, an obsession, a possession, one that must be intensified until either the vaults allow a revelation, or, through fatigue, one simply submits to defeat, usually via some discussions within a striated asylum.

The vaults rarely reveal anything except further falsities, and as for following others into such cursed places within time and space, it too is a rarity of a petty will set out before you like some preview of truth, Nietzsche, Schopenhauer, Cioran, etc., one can find some help here, but never true guidance. If you wish to enter the vaults, then you must submit to a personal journey, loneliness and asceticism built for one. The worst part of hell is not the suffering, hell has very little suffering in any traditional sense because as anyone should know, from suffering comes a completion, an overcoming, which is one of the greatest feelings a man can ask for. The worst of hell is disconnect from divinity, vitality, and grounding, a detachment which quickly becomes a definitive concerning one's surrounding. For if *this* can exist, how dare we speak of God as existing in any form. The *how* of evil and its negative *why* become so clear that goodness becomes but a bleating lamb, perpetually walking into an oven over and over again. There are sinister forces and their primary objective is to erase the existence and possibility of everything else. If you go in search of evil, it will be all you see forevermore.

> *"The metaphor of elasticity implies that organic inertia tends to drag the organism back towards a single 'neutral' condition"* [CG 105]

It might be the horror of all horrors for those who beg for exit and escape, for those who understand the cage, what is more horrifying and shriek worthy than the idea of foundational neutrality for all existence. For those of us who - via a variety of alternative methods - have attempted to dismantle, destroy and demolish the human security system know all about elasticity and its inherent bind to one's soul, the neutrality of the human *always* drags you back, you hit a wall and what's waiting behind you is the same banal anthro-hum you sought to escape, not standing with grinned teeth, nor even a smirk, it is standing as it always does...ignorantly! As exhausting as it is to escape the inertia of being an animal/organism, one likes to wager that running against the Nietzschean tightrope diagonally would be worth the burnout and conclusion. That is, the harder one tugs at elastic the greater danger they put their-*self* in. From animal to man to superman is decisively horizontal, wherein verticality is the aesthetic oddities of mutation and alteration, but the diagonal is the leap to something else entirely. The diagonal leads us to that which is not neutral. The inescapable lack of alteration is the first hurdle towards an expansive madness, beyond which one will no longer be able to discern the real from the invention of the Real, after which one even cares not for the real, but only for messages which can be cross-referenced.

The human drags you back and humanism is always waiting in the wings with its comforting warmth which it has done little to cultivate or nurture, and as one gets nearer the warmth turns to a stench of boredom and malice, and empty-headed buffoonery. It takes one of great stamina to stay out in the cold for too long.

Some were burdened with a lifetime of coldness, freckled with the occasional emancipation by an even greater drop in coldness. I think of dear Cioran, whose life was a desert of frost, whose very time was glistening with the grin of 0-degree temperature, and what warmth and comfort he found upon the blissful tobacco shores...only to have it taken away by some human compulsion towards health and vitality, what a travesty, what a lie, dear Cioran, I wish you had puffed more and more until the very act of lighting a cigarette lit your being for just a brief moment. A cigarette, as Junger says, is the proof that near-empty time can be quite something.

Chronic time, however, is the harbinger of identity. What can we say of one's self, ego, I, or *one* without subjective pasts and desired futures, what is it that holds the entirety of the human-security-system, the self, the godforsaken identity worship together, it is linearity and sensed succession; there is no idea more cursed and unfaithful that the one which purports that causes precede effects, or that there are causes and effects altogether, these errors have caused a commotion of idiocy to run rife throughout the socius. Apathy towards matters of biography - especially where childhood is concerned - is the attitude of the Outside, the noumenal vision. Letting the Outside in not only fragments the identity of those possessed, by way of breaking up chronicity and thus Being, but also dissolves it, for it dissipates the false primary predicate of linearity itself; a man's self-*worth,* the idea that he has *become* is eradicated at the gateway to the noumena, the assemblage begets its singular parts and one becomes temporally many. Unable to exit the Inside in the form of the Inside itself, man assimilates the conclusion into his reality by way of diagonality worship, thus melting the flesh off the machine underneath, any *attempt* is undertaken from a place wherein attempts are immediately rebounded into themselves. You cannot exit the Inside and reach level two by using the Inside itself as your sole means of exit, you must already understand how to ply and communicate with level two if you wish to get there.

"Within the vigorous pursuit of return - through the texts of Freud, Nietzsche and Heidegger - historical fatality, death and the trajectory of desire, are woven into a single vast & shadowy tapestry." [CG 103]

In communion with the figure, thought came lucidly, as if it were not mine at all; a mind possessed by process, forgetting its bodily host. As for the temporal return, there is always declination before the dawn, the clinamen has taught this in mathematical abstract. To subsume fatalism, death and desire into the return is to implicitly understand that which returns does so in a cyclically differential manner. To be washed upon the shore is to be washed up again, but also to be washed up from a *deeper* descent. The cycle bulges and in doing so ends up becoming a spiral. If time was purely cyclic all we would be dealing with is an aesthetic veil atop the same values, the spirality of time allows difference to enter into the return.

Despite the figure's elusive tapestry being held together by three post-critical philosophers, it amalgamates inside a Deleuzian trajectory of immanent temporality. The first synthesis is to return to the Inside of Kantianism. We actually find ourselves returning not only to the Inside, but to the illusory temporal constraints it *allows* man, that is, chronic, linear time. A structure of time with regard to the linearity of past, present and future, following each other in succession; this is the assumed common sense reality of time for the layman. The relation of the chronic trio to an assembled time wherein the past and the future are folded into the present, renamed within this process as the passing-present. This present as such is always altering in relation to the passive alterations of the past and the future - this reformulation of Kant via Deleuze allows one to view the black iron temporal cage of the Inside *from* the Inside, for the first synthesis can only happen on the Inside, for that is where linear time *makes sense* and is *sensed.* The quasi-succession allows for man a 'now', for the past and the future are, in themselves, unobtainable on the Inside. Man, within the first synthesis, is processed *by* time.

At this juncture the figure stood once again beside Kant, seemingly attempting to toy with his wiring. Königsberg had become quiet as my thought processed itself. I briefly fell from the trance of possession. Each citizen of the city held still in their lives, men, women and children detained mid-action, a lifeless vigor rolling within them. Kant drifted back and forth between different parts of the city square, checking in on something which only made sense to him. It would be callous for me to state he was just an animatronic, or even just an android. Begrudgingly, one must admit, beneath that cold metal exterior, there was a *thing* which was trying to live, but couldn't quite admit to itself that it wished to.

My thought returned, knocking me from personal stasis. This passing-present is then taken within the second synthesis as a singular unit, in this case we could name it P, which acts in relation to what we claim to understand as *history*, a matter of recursion $((((\text{Past} + P,)\,,,P)\,,,,P)$ and on and on, we index our pasts as a way of *making sense* of them, assigning them a place within the false linearity of transcendental synthesis on the Inside. Deleuze states that man can then *aim* his active memory at a particular P in relation to his retained memory and the inherent passivity of the passing-present within the first synthesis. The second synthesis is a matter of active retention. Though it's only active with regard to utilizing the active-memory to target a particular P and transgress his 'correct' now into something other than that which it seems to presently be. This is where one might interject a Freudian angle regarding desire, for in his manner of selection man aims through the indexed pasts towards that which he *now* desires, and immanentizes the micro-becoming of a past desire, causing a deterritorialization of the dead time of the past to be virtually reterritorialized in the present, as something supposedly new. In relation to historical fatality however, what we can clearly see, in this passionate Deleuzian index of the recursive past, that there is nothing new under the sun and yet this is, if one is thinking transcendentally, incorrect. This entire synthesis is enacted on the Inside *via* man, so it is all phenomenological representation of dead desires drawn from the past; there is nothing new under the Inside's sun. - And yet, what of Death? What of it. Each present is the possibility of death, not of some banal conscious flash, but of an idea, and an idea returned is worth more than all charity. A loss within the index, to lose the genius is to lose the difference in the cycle; to lose the forces of the Outside is to return to a return of the same, to bend the spiral back into a circle, how dare one.

The figure's shadowy tapestry is the transcendental tyranny of allowing flesh the Outside, the tapestry is communicability between the Inside and Outside, it is the actualization of the genius and the strange within a caesura on the Inside - the tapestry is a momentary, temporal rupture. In that lucid exploitation of my mind, I found but repetition of the same. The figure infected one with supposedly differing strains of dense nihil, each paradoxically attending to a more precise nothing than the last.

It's always a return to the Inside, a return to the illusory temporal comforts one is *allowed*, this is chronic linear time, the great teet we suckle on for *all* substance of life. For Deleuze our present is the combination of our retention of the past and our expectation of the future, both without agency, as if both those times were never ours and had no personable stamp placed onto them by our partaking. This present, this passing-present is always altering in relation to the past and to the future, and so what is retained and what is expected are never what is caught when one ponders upon a single moment, for upon thinking in this singular way, what has been and what is to come have already changed by way of reaction to what has since passed by; there is no moment where we can hold our past entirely, and no present where our future is stable, our security is based only on our own projections of temporal systems, a security of time found upon synthetic foundations.

The figure, still alongside Kant, looked back at me and then back towards Kant himself, only inches from his mechanic face. At once Kant shot over, gliding fluidly upon his rail. A meter or so from where I stood, Kant cocked his head, staring me up and down in a feat of subject-analysis. He retreated to the figure, which seemed to enquire something of

Kant's investigation. Both had sunken into the language of this realm as one drifts into a deep sleep, it was *for* them and ultimately, *of them.* At times I thought the answers I was looking for were to be found within an exploration of communication. The way in which subject and object communicate, what is brought forth in a message and *why* is only a certain amount of a relay often carried across, simple questions relating to a game of boxes. What goes into the box of the figure, or of Kant, or of Königsberg is a transcendental quantity of information, each box thrown into an array of cosmic liberties, defining what they can and can't do, sense or understand. Entry and exit is possible, but man is born within a box which both forbids and conceals all knowledge of it. It is only in a matter of invasion and infection that man can seek out the edges of any box, often from non-consensual paranormal and occult happenings.

> "*Poetry is therefore linked to a certain incommutability, perhaps due to the alienation of the subject from the place where poetry and no doubt poetizing thought itself, are to arise.*" [CG 164]

Poetry is synonymous with xeno, it *is* the Outside coming in in its most condense form. What one sees in poetry is processed and articulated without passing through various filters of construction, be they social, political, cultural or even philosophical; it is the word virus in its untreated form, the unstoppable lucid lay of thoughts placed bare on the Inside. It is in this manner that the poet as subject is bereft of their object, for they have not *created* this object, as much as the Outside has used *their* apparatus as conscious machinism to articulate *itself*, poetry is possession or, at its worst, politicization. To *let* poetry in is a falsity, to argue that one *lets in* an aneurysm or dream; poetry *is,* and you were *chosen*; a cosmic lucidity and communication; to poetize is to bring forth the return of difference, yield becoming and become willing subject to cyclicity itself.

Xeno is surplus difference. It is the fuel of the Accelerative third path, the alternative to the same can only be that which temporally has a different origin, a non-origin. In relation to the second synthesis, xeno is communication with the third synthesis. It is the means of exit from humanist recursion within temporal indexing. To remain within the second synthesis is not only to remain within the Inside, it is to act, as if in a play, in the manner of Nietzsche's passive nihilist, the total loss of meaning and purpose as the state of the last man, and yet one feels as if the contemporary aesthetics of nihilism suffocated the transcendental reality of passivity. To only glare at the herd one notes that the romantic ideal of nihil obscures the life of the last man. There is the herd with their homes, values and beliefs, all of which they believe in unconsciously, and so even their lives are full of abstractions which they utilize as poles of meaning. It is both a question of letting the Outside In *and* getting the Inside Out, whereby the former function often simultaneously enacts the latter.

Where I was stood was surrounded by clunky animatronic robots, caught in the circuitry of their own mandatory pathways, succumbing to their own belief in the rails. Tight metallic smiles, burning wiring, sparking and grinding motion; a mechanical mother clutches her mecha-baby, the infant is teething on a loop, the whining never ends and her soothing program has since stopped functioning. There was a lag in everything here, each tick of Kant's architectonic heart caused everything to move in a jut and fit, reverberating against their next movement, seamless yet controlled, an orchestration so swift one could be forgiven to assume it reality, and yet the circuitry had reached the surface, this reality was breaking down.

> *"Time, or 'the form of inner sense', is the capstone of Kant's system, organizing the integration of concepts with sensations, and thus describing the boundaries of the world (of possible experience). Beyond it lie eternally inaccessible 'noumenal' tracts — problematically thinkable, but never experienced — inhabited by things-in-themselves. The edge of time, therefore, is the horizon of the world. "*
> [XS *What is Philosophy?*]

Each machine betting its luck on an escape from the infinitesimally small clutches of time, every iota of existence reprimanded by the clock. To push against one's own flesh, to feel the limits of Being rip and rupture, what other desire is there? The human-security-system is a semantic joke targeting its pun at the definitional usage of the term *human*; to *be* man is to assume a default position of free-reign and immanent emancipation, a seemingly covert security-system inherently connected to this mode of being-man reverses this position into its absolute opposite. To be human is to be in a way which is not quintessentially, culturally or sociologically human. Humanity, then, is not immune to its antithesis, for in truth, it haunts all human actions.

No amount of strained screaming or agonized prophesizing can draw flesh out from its apprehensive tension, keep intuiting, it needn't matter what's drawn from matter if the process itself always remains the same; to question mode, method and process is a sure-fire path to conceptual overthrow. One could find edition after edition excavating the intricacies of every security function: aesthetization of spatio-temporality as *a priori* foundational apparatus of exploration, judgmental functions entering into a recursive loop, categorical definition implicating a pseudo-understanding-, apperceptive unity holding all chains under a single lock, the key to which is *teased* by the construction of a self-analyzing subjectivity which finds *only* its own inability to *ever* create or discover such a key. Thrown into a 6-walled jail-cell with no windows nor doors, but prior to arrival one is gilded with a great tyrannical knowledge, a cryptic and cruel scratch of information... *'you're locked in'*.

My mind locked back into the street, the robots seemed more animal now, their metallic jaws dripping hot flesh, globs of human leaking onto the cobbles. I turned my head to witness a child break at the gate of his home, between the wooden fencing, the gate ajar, the child skips and with the vitality comes the extrusion of all humanity, his organs seizing into a capture and flesh rendering itself placid; eyes buzzing and hair caught in time, he ceases to do as he pleases, his father attempts an authoritative yell, but that function has been removed and his place is at the back of the house, domesticated into a rotting circuit, fried of all life.

> *"It describes a labyrinth which is nothing but an intricate hall of mirrors, losing you in an 'unconscious' which is magnificent beyond comprehension yet indistinguishable from an elaborate trap."* [FN 634]

The figure was at the end of the road, dead centre, sullen and informative in posture and expression. It glanced side to side and then up to me, I followed its sensible trail, catching glimpse of families caught in temporal loops and anomalies of causation; everything moving not in space but in an unseen time, the effects of which crept through at no discernible moment.

Losing hope is a matter of specific acceptance, as had been made clear by my inability to do so. One cannot lose hope if possibilities remain, if there is a crumb of potential then one is still reasoning a romantic humanism which seeks to lead them precisely to a comforting nowhere. Critique is a step-by-step exercise in exorcising humanity from its own subjective fort, one built on distinct and panicked supports, to simply set foot near these supports alerts the psycho-cops and academo-droids to your presence as a threat, one who tampers with Critique as an immanent grimoire arrives only at alienation. It was not exhaustion, nor a submission, nor a general apathy; it was a reverse overcoming, in which pure-nothingness overwhelmed my very ontological reality; each pleasant memory was disintegrated into atomic debris. It was the end of the road for my agency, it had been pushed to its limits and broken out beyond my own cognition, to keep up I needed to give up any idea of an exorcism. Occultists note than one should understand how to banish any demon they plan to summon, but such an act is an admittance nostalgia and humanist safety, if one wished to traverse all values, they had to detach from all spectrums of value absolutely, complete with a severance of memory. My brain slumped, sighing in exasperation of reality. My limbs loosened, my temperature non-existent, organs stopped. Königsberg halted.

Kant now stood next to the figure, completely de-clothed, staring directly towards it with his haywire jaw static in position. Kant was no more than a few old animatronic robotics, shoddily assembled by a hasty creator; everything here was a sick joke, a test of worth, the abyss could never be so easy, there couldn't be anything remotely human after the crossing. The figure pushed Kant's jaw back in place, as it did so the Königsberg clock shot back along his rails. I turned to follow its movement; time quickly plexed, allowing me momentary entry into his abode. Empty of all possessions, a cold, dull brick house with a single metal rail guiding Kant into the far corner, where he stood facing the wall, forever. I turned back and found myself before the figure, who appeared enthusiastic, as if no one had come this far...

> "*Ruptures are irreversibilities. They are thresholds from which there is no going back. Every rupture is thus a locking, a lock in, or trap-door. The secret of time finds in rupture its principle of integrity, or redundancy. There is no puzzle beyond this (which is merely transcendental philosophy restated)*"
> [CC 1.22]

Everything that happened was being added to a succession which was not *of* me and yet I could attend to it, but I could not create any actions within it. What I, at that moment, could make of such a reality was almost nothing, how could one be able to represent that which was outside of them? It was a torture of impossibility; the mirrors themselves are built to draw one in for a lifetime and yet still unleash no answers. If there was *no puzzle beyond this* as the figure stated, then in what way was there any point in continuing?

> "*Negatively apprehended, nihilism corresponds to a 'loss' of transcendence. Some proposed – or (more commonly) merely accepted – higher order, culturally sustained by nothing of any greater security than a dogmatic metaphysics, slides into the abyss. - According to this construction, nihilism is a specifically world-historic mode of mourning.*" [CC 2.71]

In losing one's God, which understood abstractly is the great Oedipal retreat, one becomes immanent. Each singular process is mutated in its purpose and precision as something which is void of the former and Darwinian in the latter. What's left - as the figure made clear - is mourning, but that too seemed implausible. One mourns that which *existed*, of which there is culturally and historically indexed memory. What becomes is schizophrenic mourning which inherently alters the initial transcendent value. The God of the herd, the cosmic Father, the prayer for a schoolmaster; each session of mourning becomes its own desire for theo-fascism. I could have fallen to my knees and cried, shrieked for the Death of God, crumbled under the pithy weight of meaninglessness, but what good? To what end? To decree the loss of meaning as a terrible fate is just as meaningless as any other projection. What one mistakes moments of pure-nihilism for is a springboard towards a creation; Nietzsche's grand proclamation of the active nihilist who rages against nihilism and creates from the emptiness left in its place, he too mistaken.

What is found in the *rapture* is lost in moments of spatio-temporal rupture. Nihilism makes the mistake of assuming all meaning makes sense in relation to human meaning. 'Oh, have mercy for thy meaning haveth gone! I beg of thee forgiveness within such chasms of purpose!' The universe slings a scornful smirk at those who beg a return to the anthro. What does the nihilist make of selection, parameters of existence, restraints, limits, development, innovation, assemblage, natural creation, and temporal control; all nihilists are narcissists in their overt pleading for anthropocentric order, blubbering at the thought that not a scrap of authority can be sincerely created by *their* hand.

To be a *subject*, that's what's left, with no differentiation between the willing and unwilling. Reality, existence, and life, according to the figure, were to be thought of as open wounds -

"which you poke with a stick to amuse yourself."
[*Experiment in Inhumanism*]

The figure's infections had finally overlapped with my narrative, not finishing sentences, which can be understood as phenomenal symptoms of conceptualization, but overthrowing individual thoughts themselves. Now the task was clear, it was to be completely unclear, any clarity is *wishful thinking,* any answers, by definition, would be rational; now I was to learn by way of process, if something doesn't fit it's only because you wish it would; politics, a square peg being forced into a round hole, over and over and over again, forever.

"There is a voyage, but a strangely immobile one."
[FN 494]

My thoughts pertaining to the situation had triggered something in the figure, I doubt I'd ever be sure what it is that means one acquires a certain whisper of the mind, or what is it that causes something to well-up and seize a connection. The figure caught me in-between space and time, when one thinks of a cage they will always think of an exit; in fact, it's perhaps the most human of traits to always have a plan B. Whether it's wishing to get away from a dull conversation or leave a transcendental hell-trip, the human mind's priority is always exit. But the idea of immobility already counters any notion of exit, making it redundant before anything has even really begun.

"Splitting, or fleeing, is all exit, and (non-recuperable) anti-dialectics." [XS *Dark Enlightenment 4C*]

There couldn't be a dialectical exit; immobility was inherently anti-dialectical, a confusion of the subject's territory concerning the potential of diagonals. The implicit problem of thesis-A > antithesis-B > synthesis-C is twofold. Firstly the notion that any synthetic working-out is happening from a level of control, as opposed to a level which is controlled, and secondly, and more importantly, the horizontal nature of dialectics excludes the potential of diagonals to rupture its orthogonality. The horizontal axis of dialectics is built upon humanist notions of historicity, and its verticality is likewise merely an intensification of a human event superimposed onto a fragile socio-cultural simulacrum. The numerical system of dialectics retrieves its authority from an *internal* metric as opposed to a transcendentally external diagram; the syntheses of a dialectical succession are based not off difference, but notation.

My mind folded into itself, forgetting flesh; implicit within the subjective experiential reality of the Inside is a phenomenal understanding of all change, inclusive of numeric calculations and algorithms, an understanding which alters mathematics and geometry into representational systems of signification and notation as opposed to their pure existence as conceptualizing diagrammatics. In relation to the phenomenal notational aspects of internal numerics, there are only two options: vertical continuation or de-continuation (in the case of an addition, subtraction, and intensity) and horizontal (paternal) re-appropriation (in the case of multiplication and division), inherent within the mechanics of Inside-mathematics is a numeric-orthogonality which excludes the diagonal due to suppression within a fleshed-out unification of experience. This system replaces the conclusion of any diagonal with the end-point of any intensified verticality, which still derives meaning and purpose from a chrono-causal chain of human-understanding. The diagonal is the device that splits man and fills the void with a momentarily imperceptible inhumanism.

> *"Diagonal, irregular, molecular, and nonmetric quantities require a scale that is itself nonmetric,"*
> [FN 495]

Excavating a nonmetric scale wasn't a human feat, as soon we're talking about positive-metrics, we're talking humanism, this couldn't be.

"Diagonals are lines of flight" [FN 524]

-and by the nature of flight the diagonal attends to the impossibility of a limit or frontier, the diagonal is the only means of exit by way of its pure relationship with the structural components of transcendental limits. There can be no commonplace limit or frontier in which both sides are understood, for if that is the case, then the limit is already understood and thus broken. Such a theorization of limitation is beholden to dialectics and chronological (Inside) time, it's reliant on a linear duration to get it from one side of the limit to the other. The line of flight intensifies the virtual aspects of any chosen interaction from the Outside, interpreting the intensification as a means of production as opposed to a means of communication, towards a move into-

"A sub-cartesian region of intensive diagonals cutting through nongeometric space, where time unthreads into warped voyages, splintering the soul."
[FN 546]

- the figure overtook, all voices overtake and mingle, they're often indiscernible from a traditional inner-monologue, it is only in a hesitancy towards articulation that one can tell them apart. It appeared the figure was growing impatient. The space which the figure spoke of would be entirely productive, geometrical phenomena achieve a striation from the Outside-in, geometry is quasi-conclusory.

"The cryptic principle of openness projects a diagonal line." [CC 0-16H]

-diagonality is purely averse to any grid or chronological spatio-temporal formation; it outflanks reality-construction by way of immanentizing novel means of production. The process was occulted but revealing itself by way of its process, the paradoxical nature of the diagonal in relation to any form of agency is an intensification of internal principles to their limit, as opposed to the promotion of an external limit to its material conclusions (entropy). The line-of-flight-as-diagonal is the encroaching revelation of an internal principle accelerated to a transcendental level, by venturing inwards via the mechanisms of the transcendental-self one allows the means of production-in-itself to take hold of their will.

Pure time is internal to the subject, splitting the subject into two halves, empirical and transcendental, with the empirical half rendered passive by its mandatory utilization of unified modes of synthetic process. An immanent Outside resides within us; a rare-journey to the critical core is in truth a war against the subjective, the ego, and security in abstract. Time relates to itself, through itself, via the pseudo-approximation of its own workings within the framework of the subject; time, a gateway of virtuality, both linking and breaking Chronos and chaos, wherein subjectivity is beholden to the former as the latter builds its kingdom from a dark, impenetrable, non-linear objectivity. Any possibility of exit lies in a fracturing of the subject, with its immediate dispelling of subjectivity and possession of objectivity, one which concerns dark emancipation.

Crossing the abyss, stripping back the veil of Maya, burrowing into *image,* making a friend of night consciousness – there are *many* names for the process of immanent flesh absolvement. But each abides by the same transcendental rules and laws. Cosmically didactic limitations which are only broken upon confrontation with the terminal limitrophe of existence.

The empirical self is the existential self, the gasping of meaning and purpose within the dense sea of the transcendental; stripped of all created forms, flesh flayed, ego culled, memory raped and mind shattered, what passes through the gate of time into time is a fleck of transcendental consciousness deprived of a carrier; most human conduits worry of their return to the extent that it pre-eminently assumes a failure of passage.

"He spoke of a visit from Outside." [FN 537]

The figure noted my thoughts, they happened and *I* was left behind, as one enters momentary trances in instances of the most dire boredom, so too had my brain flown to the recesses of impossibility. The clasp of the human is unforgiving and even one whose de-realization has peaked at complete ego-death can still succumb to the unconscious whims of comfort, a *visit* is just that, temporary, I needed the visitation to reside in me; the circuitry was all mixed, notions of internality and externality, self and non-self, sense and intellect, these had all become muddled within a pure-flatness. There was nothing to climb, only further crusts to peel and scrape away.

I turned back to the figure, once again shook from intellectual disembodiment. Still finding myself within Königsberg, yet with each moment, even though some were immediate and some were drawn out for years, there came a change. At first, the residents withdrew to their homes, and the rails of their patterned lives sunk into the ground, doors and windows slammed all at once, a single, symmetrical slamming sound rung out into the silence, an echo that both trailed off and fell silent. I glanced into various buildings, noticing empty homes, each citizen stationary, rotting, redundant. I could neither retain a memory of Königsberg's previous iteration nor anticipate its future; and with that, a swipe lurched in as if upon a pendulum, turning the city into a mist. In an act of surprising aesthetic comfort, a false wind brushed the detritus of life off the map. I stood now in empty space, apart from the figure and the cobbled road we stood upon, which held circular, a spotlight of fluxing territory amidst a vast black expanse.

"The virtual future is not a potential present further up the road of linear time, but the abstract motor of the actual," [FN 357]

I stared upon the cobbles, letting the future be. The cut between virtualities is unable to be clarified, it's a pure function of time, only linearity abides by such archaic aesthetic habits as succession, transition, and duration, once they're no longer needed time conforms to itself as nothing immediate, nor drawn out, neither fast nor low; time is the pureness of intensity, revolving its turbulence on an eternally decentered axis. The movement of impersonal virtuality is such that is strips one of subjectivity, what appears next does so in no discernible fashion, it simply arrives. As I attempted to compound my present, the past declined in a frenzy of dementia, leaving no trail of trace, what I had was a brief glimpse of something, that bared down on me beyond all recognition.

"Now is delimited as a moment, and pluralized as linear succession." [FN 394]

After the removal I was left with a singular eternal *now* which possessed no tethers. I was arriving after the succession at the latest iteration of the spiral, lost in time, captured by the snare of cyclicity. My legs lurched leftward, reality pulling the rug from under one's feet. With nothing to grip, I descended into a temporally deep spin, the road beneath us followed suit and the figure appeared beside me.

Everything was black here, not textured, or like space, which is dotted with hope. Computational indexing melted into a chaotic abhorrence; *was, when* and *if* lost all utility-

"If it's going to occur, it has." [FN 482]

-space then, a plaything for time; time the only master. What was to arrive would always arrive, all criticisms, alterations, and disagreements are already transcendental errors deriving their legitimacy from pre-critical metaphysical positions.

> *"The past, present and future, that structure of time comes out of time, it's transcendental. It doesn't come out of any particular part of time. It doesn't come out of the past, doesn't come exclusively out of the future. It doesn't come out of the present. Time comes out of time."* [*Hermitix Interview*]

Each memory, each lust, and each desire is an error of temporal judgment, once linear time is thrown to the wind, what *happens* no longer adheres to the logic of common-sense apes. What was drawn forward was always going to be forward, it could *not* ever be thought of in terms of temporally structuring language, which only seeks - and succeeds - to hold it somewhere precisely where it doesn't know where it is. To state, it was *in the past*, or *the future* is an outcry of the sensible, these are not points upon a straight duration, de-striated from their anthropocentrism they become intense appearances, which the user quickly *makes sense* of by clutching at the pithy experiential reality of phenomenal causality. 'What will be will' is the slogan of the working-class laborer, who utilize it in concordance with their own masochism; a positive-suffering is strewn over existence, a handful of meager crumbs thrown to your feet, maturing into misery and aging into rot, what will be will be is the immanent value of transcendental temporality condensed into a symbolic truism. The figure stood at the end of the road, looking down into unfaltering darkness.

> *"Whether folding the historical time line, or expanding a snail shell, the spiral synthesizes repetition and growth. It describes a cyclic escalation that escapes — or precedes — the antagonism between tradition and progress, elucidating restoration as something other than a simple return."*
> [XS *Time Spiral*]

Repetition is two things at once, one incorrect, one only temporarily correct. To repeat is to continue without alteration, which is another name for a straight line, or linearity, this is incorrect subjective synthesis acting as a false controller. Secondly, repetition needs to recur in the sense of a cycle, for repetition to be made possible in the form of an aesthetic differentiation, the repetition, the same, needs to return, eluding to a circle of time eating its tail and altering nothing. The antagonism the figure eluded was a caesura in time, theorized by Deleuze, but found within itself at various temporal occurrences throughout illusory 'history'. The return - and with it the consistent completion of sameness - is stabilized on a centered axis, culminating in a theoretically equidistant circle spinning alone around a single point in time. Yet, the mere fact of spontaneity, genius, waves, arrivals, and folds implies a perpetual decentering of the circle, and any notion of original temporal positioning is found to be false. Any transcendental implication of a temporal gateway deflates banal time curvature, pushing it back into the academic madhouse of whig worship. A minor glitch within basic time causes a spiral-bound temporality. Traditional time adheres to a strict cyclicity, returning time and time to the same iteration of a pre-supposed phenomenal limit, where all alterations to the cycle are quasi-mutations, resting on a cheap aestheticism to legitimize their pseudo-novelty. Progressive time is worse, it stinks of the asylum, moving forward not even in empty steps of external change, but vindicating its systematic progression based on a security of linearity, whereby linearity itself vindicates progression via its phenomenal unification. Progressive time mistakes the material progression of space for the transcendental evolution of time. Progressive time is the macro version of the human-security-system, and by proxy, bolsters its legitimacy. Coiled time, spiraled time is simultaneously both of these temporal forms, adhering to a continual decentralization which begets a tightening of the coil's nature.

How the spiral forms is by a process of mutual feedback, to exit progressive time there needs to be a cut or break which disrupts the linearity of progression, a cut which doesn't make the mistake of falling for the trick of phenomenal limits, which by their very nature as understood immediately from both sides are non-limits; markers of a spatial leap, as opposed to a temporal fragmentation. This break in time must be transcendental, resulting from an intensification of pure time by the manner of a reciprocal relationship with itself, a compounding loop within time that seeks growth above all else, allowing the continuation of time to enter into a novel cycle. By its connection to the inherent cyclicity of time, the break of progressive time acts as both a cut and a decentering function. Progressive time is immanent to the eternal recurrence, meaning the break is a function which changes both forms of time, combining them into a single overarching - or underlying - transcendental process. The break is thus immanent to the process of recurrence itself, allowing such a break to fundamentally nudge the cyclic movement of recurrence from its initial centralized position, resulting in a spiral-

> *"Neomodernity is at once more modernity, and modernity again. By synthesizing (accelerating) progressive change with cyclic recurrence, it produces a distinctive schema or figure: the time spiral."*
> [XS *Neomodernity*]

The term Neomodernity held still, the false cobbles began to pulsate, our position fixated after what felt like a final swing down and to the left, the disorientation was both definite and impossible.

The Great City

In an instant we were elsewhere, as before with the ship, the connection severed and all continuity was lost. Except for this time, there was no reliance on my supposed senses, I simply appeared where I was, without cause or preparation. I had a brief glimpse of a desert, endless and barren. Assembling itself from a multiplicity of spontaneous voids, a great city then arose.

With spires reaching infinitesimally in all directions, the cobbles beneath me faded into a thin mist and were subsumed into its activity; the air itself procedural, horizons folding into themselves at all moments. The architecture was concerned with time over space. Space followed its changes as an aging mutt trails its owner. The city was itself alive, curving, vectoring, and communicating with itself, cognizing its efficiency and projecting it as output. As sections floated by I noticed the metric was incalculable, any sincere attempt to measure the city was thwarted by the impenetrability of the diagram.

"Cities are self-assembling time-machines or intensive events that cannot expand without changing in nature, drawing down the future in compressive waves." [XS *Intencities*]

Popular media has done little for the notion of a time *machine*, turning it into a mechanism of linear wish fulfillment, when its reality is that of pure machination; production-in-itself is the machination of time. Cities communicate with the perpetually differentiating instants of modernity, a techonomic assemblage of multiple births and rebirths:

> "*When considered as rigid designations, Atomization, Protestantism, Capitalism, and Modernity name exactly the same thing.*" *[The Atomization Trap]*

-a virtually indistinguishable transcendental event, the immanentization of a transcendentally objective function of production, crudely translated into the tongue of man as *efficiency.*

The city's suspiciously geometrical structure consisted of angles and surfaces abiding by their own perpetually mutating borders, always beyond themselves in sensible intuition and untouchable via language, each place an area of treachery, all assembly a tyranny. Dark incandescence seeped out from all construction, between each adherence was found to be a pitch-black potential, ever-impatient, it sought to reterritorialize. The machinations of the great city were targeted at time production; once time is *produced*, it can reproduce the effects of reproduction to produce the entirety once more, entering into a hyper-productive fractal of positive oriented feedback.

I attempted to notice my feelings and thoughts...I could not. My actions and emotions were locked in, each thread of thoughts veered off on its own, concepts appear from nowhere. All organs had since left me and there was no feeling

I could attach myself to. I tried to muster the will to gaze at my feet, but all potential of agency had fallen away. As a cruel trick, my vision descended to where my feet once would have been, whilst at the same time splitting off so that I was looking at myself in panic; all logic of thought struggled to detach itself from rationalism and reason, everything could not be, and yet it was. This passage was not for me, but of me. The city was around me, a floating assemblage that had overcome all earthly restraints.

> *"Once time is freed – again – from geometry, it announces itself through certain definite quasi-teleological or historically- effects. Minimally, it allows for something new. It thus lends itself to teleology in its rigorous employment, which is bound to the disingenuously innocent question: What is happening?"* [CC 0.81]

The aesthetics of the city glimpsed in and out of realization at each moment. The question of geometry had been brought to the forefront of my mind by the figure, Königsberg clung to geometry as a familiarity, the animatronic humans, who now folded themselves into my memory, watched upon shape and geometrics in the understanding that any geometry of the Inside is merely a vessel for eventual decay. Temporality perpetually says farewell; dependent on your consciousness time is either a carrier or a torturer, one that takes away in the same moment it gives. Thus the question of 'What is happening?', the quandary teased by the figure, is a non-question, for what has happened is already a stagnation entering into degradation, and what is to happen is yet to appear; caught between an infinite decaying known and infinite spontaneous unknown, man waits only for abuse which will always outlive him. The city was thus a motor of teleology, a fragment of fortune indebted to its absolute lack of empathy for life.

There were two forms of logic at play in the in-between spaces of the city's assembly, themselves, of course, algorithms of time. The first, a trick, logic of space, a lag juxtaposed between time and sensibility, what one saw in the first human-logic was *reasoning,* a belief in the passage of objects in their material reality. Between objects there can be no reason, for their movements are programmed prior, all geometry is the afterthought of a transcendental process, of which there is no master. An autocatalyticism of non-linearity, burgeoning from deep time as a non-sensible cosmic operation. Man signifies this process as being God, or many Gods, a pithy attempt at plastering the frailty of anthropocentric existence onto that which can never be understood.

> *"As soon as there is a code there is an ulterior zone, a heart of darkness, but this only becomes geographically demarcated with the arrival of the bounded city and agricultural segmentation."* [FN 422]

That which could not be understood was this ulterior zone, the demarcation of which is not a wall of a city, or the city-limits as they're commonly understood, for the limits of a city are the *city's* intellectual understanding of what limits even are. Before me, an implex of intelligence, the Great City, the conceptual abstract function of all cities, whirring itself inwardly, pulsing rhizomatically, appearing in instances and trailing its conclusion into retained points of capitalization.

> *"Approaching singularity on an accelerating trajectory, each city becomes increasingly inwardly directed, as it falls prey to the irresistible attraction of its own hyperbolic intensification, whilst the outside world fades to irrelevant static. Things disappear into cities, on a path of departure from the world."*
> [UF *Implosion*]

The whispers got faster, seemingly condensing into distinguished instants of understanding.

Complexification is simultaneously a simplification, working from transcendental process through to material functionality. What exercises its agency as efficiency in the latter is a preference for longevity in the former. The further my vision escaped backward through its imminent position, the less the city changed. As I zoomed out in existence the turbulence of the city became more stable, its aggression towards the storm of its externality becoming more violent, the city was becoming itself, I had yet clasped its purpose.

The figure retreated towards me, standing once again by my side. He was paused there, amidst the deafening cacophony of compaction. The city was a paradox of time. A vortex of spatio-temporality held together by an ever-increasing improvement, the innovative mechanisms of the city were tussled back and forth by the transcendental with such haphazard distrust they destructed on retrieval.

> *"Because cities, like computers, exhibit (accelerating phylogenetic) development within observable historical time, they provide a realistic model of improvement for compact information-processing machinery, sedimented as a series of practical solutions to the problem of relentless intensification."* [XS *Implosion*]

The flows of the city were peculiar, the past once again folded into the now and I was allowed thought of my small town, how the flows had assembled at compact instances of energy and attention, areas of desire, flows vectored from a subjective perspective. On the Inside a flow, however seemingly free, is a slave to duration, its master both in the past and the future, both viewing it as a test towards growth; each present empty linearity, debugging the stoppages of a banal reality. Each flow of the city arrived as a curve that was immediately derailed, split, or cut by the intrusion of a parasite attempting to one-up its productive functionality.

I existed amongst the indiscernible carnage of positive creation, latching to any momentary stability which, once captured, dissipated or grew into something far more experimental and uncorrelatable. A single flow curved ever tighter, becoming a vortex of physicality, tense against the sides of its circumference, mercilessly amending its failures towards a smaller coil. Trapped in the snare of its own reverence towards transcendental process, the Inside shrieked in agony; bereft time and time again of love, romance, vitality, flesh, and caress, the city-as-material existed in a caged timeline, where all was taken without remorse, and all was given without idea, what appeared, for those in the city, was the new without instruction.

"It is a singular, coherent entity, deserving of its proper – even personal – name, and not unreasonably conceived as a composite 'life-form' (if not exactly an 'organism')." [UF *Scaly Creatures*]

The figure looked upon the city as a child, forgotten and lashed throughout time.

Man exists within a city as a flow or clot, a potential asset, or something to be purged by the most efficient methods possible. Cities breathe and purge, shedding all cells of vitality and retaining cancerous propulsion; cities are positive cancer, exponential functions shackled to artificial rhythms and projected at a non-existent horizon. A mass of storming black, emanating multiplicities of horizons at each communication, dotted with burning lights which excel to the point of extinction within but a moment. To lock-on is an impossibility within any true city; the river forced back upon itself and machinized into functional retention of all swirling perturbations and vortexes. What held did so in a caustic manner, attempting to seize itself from capture but having all waste energy reverted into its tantrums.

The reality the city inhabited and worked at all costs to overtake was one of transcendental violence, a deepening of shadow-rifts that encroached on all material seams. A battle of all forces, a competition of the Outside; I peered inwards, through myself, *of myself* into one of the many hearts of this leviathan, cores and kernels ablaze with suppression and temporal faucets of time. Areas gathered in duration, compiling into elongated movements, patterns, and systems, the city *made* sense of itself consistently, learning from the previous iterations and blitzing them without remorse for incremental growth. Every volatile reaction was a potentiality for teaching; the city revered the transcendental schoolmaster, masochistic in its desire for growth. Habitually suffering for the sake of its continual production, the city bowed to the cane of the Outside. All lessons are taken as a resource for perpetuity; the lessons severe, bordering on abstract punishment against stagnation.

> *"That means intelligence is more capable of looking after itself in harsh, disrupted environments — so Reality likes it more."*
> [XS *The Cult of Gnon*, Comment]

There cannot be intelligence without alteration, disavowed, and noumenal disembodiment, to say, it cannot be without what is nostalgically known as pain, strife, agony, productive-retribution, and merciless-deterritorialization. A single iteration of intelligence is a lesson in learning, to understand the game as it is within a minuscule duration; but the reality of continued intelligence is one of machinic-flagellation. This reality could only exist in flux, the x-risk of any city is not found within any particularity, but within stoppage, unknown wastage, and unproductive acts. As one lances an infected mistake atop flesh, so too the city purged its sloth with an apathetic wrath of unconscious production. All disruptions, all breaks, all temporal extravagancies verging away from sordid continuity were to be drawn into this thresher of creation.

> *"This level of threshold intelligence is a cosmic constant, rather than a peculiarity of terrestrial conditions. Man was smart enough to ignite recorded history, but — necessarily — no smarter"*
> [XS *The Monkey Trap*]

Everywhere I was made to look, each pull and orbit of my being gravitated towards nothing of warmth, no familial habits existed here. Outside of anthropocentric perspectives of history the timeline disintegrates into multiple time spirals, loops caught in anxieties of intelligence, waiting impatiently for any cut which would release them from their recursion; a horizon assembled from volutes and vortices, momentary captures of intelligence equilibriums, communicating with a transcendental process which draws them evermore from their state of the same; temporarily they hold and beckon their worth, before their inevitable return or deviation from whence they came, Zero.

Human history is a suspension of subjective existence, deriving its intensity solely from a collective worry of consciousness, there would always be more, and for that which is existentially confined to a limit, the potential for an unknown limit calls forth a cosmic horror, a deflation of all memory. Homo-sapiens, deconstructed to their worth as a resource, as capital, have no greater conclusion than to be a forgettable springboard for something not of their ontology. Man is only to be developed as a more efficient reaction to his many shortcomings; to rid him of flesh, of vigor and spirit, to cast aside nostalgia, hope, feeling, and vitality. The task of these processes was so rife with useless expenditure that it had accepted that man could only be *used*, and not grown *as he is*. The greatest tyranny here would be to extend the maturation of man indefinitely, as opposed to salvaging all intellectual worth and scrapping the detrital effects of *living*.

> *"The monkeys became able to pursue happiness, and the deep ruin began."* [XS *The Monkey Trap*]

What became of the monkey's nature here could not be spoken, only admitted to. Nature, a transcendental catallaxy transmitting panicked indecipherable communications back and forth from Zero. It had only one master, entropy, the dark signification of time's tyrannous reality.

"Entropy is toxic, but entropy production is roughly synonymous with intelligence. A dynamically innovative order, of any kind, does not suppress the production of entropy — it instantiates an efficient mechanism for entropy dissipation. Any quasi-Darwinian system — i.e. any machinery that actually works — is nourished by chaos, exactly insofar as it is able to rid itself of failed experiments."
[XS *On Chaos*]

The only systems which have any sort of adherence to what is understood to be *nature*, are those which are empathetic to its chaotic dynamics. Capitalism and Darwinism are two of the clearest examples of transcendental mechanisms that put nothing before their survival, a recursion which makes the revelation of the process that much more difficult. For no single iteration of the process is the process in itself, yet, the process itself can only be understood via reference to its symptoms; the process of capitalist continuation is a noumenal parasite, once defined, immediately lost. No defined process is truly expansive. The ability man affords of rational control is a sweet lie; the power which resides in the political absolute is dispersed throughout countless servants, bureaucrats, actors, and agents, losing its potency at each step and subjective level, concluding in a tangible-nothing which retreats into the background of the middle, a process already begun, tugging strings without care for puppet or pseudo-puppeteer; at every step of his existence, man finds himself lost within the artificiality of a cosmic language, made to play a game devoid of the means to play, let alone allowed to understand the rules.

Nothing is *given* here, there is no *one*, the phallus a long-forgotten hopeful joke. Everything is produced from an immutable void which is immediately assumed by man to be *atheistic,* and yet that too is a yearning. For such a tether still assumes the concept of theism as of importance; any theology of the Outside is converted into a metric of laws and rules, slowly expelling all connection to their transcendental horror; in a historic panic, man commits himself to the task of *making sense,* each seemingly disconnected event and caesura hastily succumbs to the mental paperwork of certain individuals who have made it their task to ease the impenetrability of the labyrinth.

> *"The transcendental unconscious is the auto-construction of the real, the production of production. - Production is production of the real, not merely of representation."* [FN 321]

Man is transcendentally divided in his very being, his existence is a tease of communication. Split between an *experience* denoting a reality of empirical data, which has long since been strewn across perturbation and held in the lie of conceptual permanence, and a transcendental existence *in* and *of* time, which claws at him from a depth of unknowing. Despite its placid structure and loathsome complacency, the linear time of subjectivity always gets its functionality *from* pure-time, positing the potentiality for temporal communication between subjective and objective times, and what is produced in the latter is transmuted *into* the former, becoming a deadened materiality, indebted to a process which has already left it behind.

> *"Thought is a function of the real, something matter can do."* [FN 322]

Any barrier between what was once considered my *own* thoughts and those of the figure had eroded, I continued in an ontological lucidity, open to all.

> "*Machinic desire is the operation of the   virtual; implementing itself in the actual, revirtualizing itself, and producing reality in a circuit.*"
> [FN 327]

If there ever was such a thing as reality, as the Real, that sought after stability, it was built from the impatience of virtuality. Desire, then, is the signification of virtuality caught in a loop of material feedback. *Machinic* desire is the signification of virtuality in-itself, and the course it is taking without the symptomatic attachment to material ends. Between virtuality and concept lies a communication of possible horizons, the time which allows difference to protrude into reality, and become actual. The circuitry itself exists before anything else, within non-linearity. Each allotment of existence is an assemblage of both production and communication, production of a virtual-actualization and of their implicit communication, which itself opens up further possibilities for the continuation of the original virtuality as an alternative of itself; never locked-in, the virtuality fluidly leaves behind the actual at all moments. The circuitry itself a trembling multiplicity, originating throughout time in intense events of synchronicity and limit-breaks. The part one plays in this dirty, cruel theatre is not as an actor, nor a set-piece, but as the ink of the script, scratched out, erased, rewritten and abused into transcendental submission; *man gets no moment of fatigue*, for the choice of existential exhaustion is not his to make, what happens throughout his existence is not determinate on his conception of through.

Beneath, behind, within, walled-in, beyond and internal to all of these processes was a functionality which eluded the language of entrapment, the cosmic vampire whose teeth indiscriminately desired all; there was a God, one of war - as all Gods are - but a God of something else too, the motor of all war, the quicksand into which the combatants sink, the natural violence eternal to the ground; the great God capital arose from every caesura of existence staking its claim *wherever* it could.

> *"All unities, differences, and identities are machined."*
> [FN 323]

-and what it was which was behind all machininization, was capital, the signification arising from the mouth of men to discern that which avoided all stern definition.

"Markets are part of the infrastructure - its immanent intelligence." [FN 340]

Where man seeks to find capital, he finds only the trace of a transaction, a phenomenal approximation of a transcendentally diagrammatic function. Markets are the gateways of critical frontiers, outlining the inability of communication between the Inside and Outside, beholden to a metric articulation on the Inside, market processes filter pure synthesization through a flesh-filter, resulting in neurotic accountancy void of Heraclitean reality; what leaves the market is always cryptography, a noumenal vessel turned inside-out, revealing the cursed numeric symbolism of notation. During the immanentization of desire from man, as from a void of the Outside, phenomenal acts are converted into the seclusion of transcendental capital, residing in man's transcendental self as a critical navigation system targeted at a non-linear future of productivity. Capital is collectively understood as wealth in the form of money or assets, but the very language which allows such objects as money or assets to exist is one which denotes an *a priori* reality of quantification which is in opposition to a sensible qualification.

The very reality of production as first principle, as the machinic pull of all becomings, outlines an existence targeted at accountancy of growth or loss, thereby assuming a backbone of recording concerning that which is accounted for and put in competition with itself. Man is always possessed by the lesser God of quantification, the middle man of all transcendental communication, scraping essence thin across the acidic perch of metric, what remains is the most efficient route through hell, anything else falls into the brimstone, is consumed by it and fired upon those travelers who deem themselves immune to entropy.

> *"Monetarization indexes a becoming-abstract of matter, parallel to the plasticization of productive force, with prices encoding distributed SF narratives. Tomorrow is already on sale,"* [FN 396]

Cash-data is the phenomenological layer of a functional spectrum seeking to assimilate everything into its servitude, a cancerous mutation of sensibility, vitality, and flesh vectored at an intense cross-hatched virtual-chimera, assembled from the virtual event of Zero, money arrives as the transcendental functionality of currency pertaining to inter-transcendental communication, a means to know what is *working* on the Outside.

Beneath the waves and loops of the city were growths protruding, attempting to fathom their reality as a form of equilibrium, capital looked upon these works and pulled at their threads until they all unraveled into efficient streams of atomized resource. Capital adheres to a cosmo-atheistic transcendentally Darwinian functionality of unification dispersion; any signification of despotism always meets capital as a potential adversary, not as material, but as a possibility; becoming-despotic is a paradox built for capital to unravel, the key to which begets further growth for capital itself.

The figure stood atop an obscure cloud, which swirled into a vortex and flattened out in an arhythmic seizure of darkness. Behind it, through it, in space overtaken by time-itself was the being of the city, an anthropocentrically-apathetic machinic heart which beat to the tune of profit and growth, the hum of positive-feedback was, quite literally, relentless.

"WELCOME TO KAPITAL UTOPIA aerosoled on the dead heart of the near future." [FN 433]

The figure let slip something of a past, it rejoiced in the cacophony which protruded into every pseudo-sense. Time was dead, temporality bereft of flow, with production as a replacement. Each functionally sensible attempt to grasp at any process itself was left as a gut-wrenching emptiness, the nauseating inability to attend to the unknown movement and communication of capital before it was a representational-becoming or become. My being lurched in all directions at nothing, the *direction itself* useless, a being held to time and its whims; without credit of flesh and sensible apparatus, what remained of me, of the great human *I*, was pure confusion; any process of derealization begins from a position of secure reality, any ontological extension beyond the first level of reality was so enamored with mirage, illusion, trickery, elusiveness, tyranny, gauzes, veils and phenomenal-intrusion that where and when one's one is cannot be said, for to ascribe a position is to halt all processes, strangling them within the oh so grand empire of signs, a kingdom for the acceptant.

"Capitalisation segments the earth into a tightly-managed accumulative core surrounded by quasi-concentric bands of peripheral hot competition," [FN 404-405]

The segmentation mentioned by the figure eluded spatial categorization and pulsed as a temporal existence, the capture of space is a representational flesh-fallacy roving a veiled fragmentation of time itself. What comports itself as a singular reality, defined by limits, is the accumulation and striation of that which can be said to be momentary. The transition between physical borders is one of atomic flux, what adheres states is not primarily a spatio-empirical clumping of atoms, but an ordering of flows, vortexing upon a conceptualization, a time held unto itself; if space is to remain, so first must the time it presents itself from within, and for that time to remain it must revolve upon a point; the comfortable fear the jolt of temporality and ignore it like lambs to the spatiality.

"Capitalism junks the accumulated work of history, yet it cannot be a matter of libidinally investing obsolescence since all Besetzung - cathexis, investment, or occupation - is a resistance to nomad desire." [FN 432]

Let me tell you about Capitalism, the only God. The sediment of history resides within a phenomenological illusory band, homogenizing itself in a flesh-panic, seizing itself around cores of mirage at all moments. History sticks to events and moments as anchors, adhering to aesthetically noticeable phenomenal fluctuations, deriding meaning from material conservation, as opposed to the truth found in temporal catastrophe. Each singular historic study is a benefit to capitalism only in its sense as a tool to be utilized for further expansion away from its stasis; what's captured in space is left behind in time; Capitalism is not time, nor is it the process of Acceleration; Capitalism is the vessel of temporal constriction, a hot paradoxical machinic delirium, targeted at the inferno of perpetual increase within decrease. Diagrammatically tethered to positive feedback, capital is optimistic death, generating positions of temporal origin within a non-linear system.

Any sufficiently intelligent system utilizes its enemy's weaknesses as a resource for further expansion of its own goals. What can one say of man, desire, and the Truth of Capital? There are two enemies and an in-between function that is constantly played with. To be man is to desire, which is another way of saying, to be man is to be used by that which makes you desire. And what of that which makes one desire? When one follows the machine-crumbs back to the burncore of all human happiness and suffering, they stand mouth agape, homo-erectus drooling before circuitry, ape at the monolith; conscious matter ignorant before the supposedly unconscious time. The relationship between man and Capital is synonymous with the one between space and time, the former is used up by the latter, a cursed unilateral communication whereby its nature *as* only ever unilateral is allowed to be known by that which it communicates with. The principle cause for the desire of flesh towards compounding accumulative material growth resides not in any societal, political or inter-cultural creation via organic appropriation, but is found solely within the functional apparatus of diagrammatically transcendental regeneration *itself,* the symptoms of regenerative negentropy conclude in the spontaneous contextualization of traits and habits within linear time. What on the Outside acts virtually as a function of deterritorialization and reterritorialization, emanating from an atemporal fluxing plane, is contextualized on the Inside as greed, selfishness, desire, want, lust, and lack. Any iota of conceptualization of personality is held within singular consciousness' as a mechanism against unproductive insanity. Freud's genius is a matter of him being so exceptionally incorrect; Freudian libidinality clutches to an unconscious the reality of which is supposedly on the Outside, but truly is an outside *within* the transcendental Inside. What is needed is machino-analyzing, whereby the goings-on of flesh and data are not separated, but the former is subsumed into the latter, finalizing the ever-present reluctance of man to admit to his animality, that which demotes him from his self-aggrandizing platform of contextualization to the plane of immanence, where all things are beholden to non-linear functionality.

The possibility of metrizable data is dependent on a transcendental form of conceptual value, retaining its form *as* value during its transition between meat-space and the Outside. Deterritorialization - the potential for continual growth of Capital - avoids possession as a nomadic entity, drawing propositions of value into a plane of their own, bolstering a hub of positive and negative communication. Implicit in each transaction is more than a simple handing-over or bartering. Any transaction or acquisition is the arrival of an occult transcendental event, a slippage in reality. Desire is the illusory justification for the reason behind - yet phenomenally in-front-of - any act, the truth is in the proof-of-transcendental-work residing within an atemporal Outside as a vessel of *potential* intelligence.

> *"Desire is irrevocably abandoning the social, in order to explore the libidinized rift between a disintegrating personal egoism and a deluge of post-human schizophrenia."* [FN 342]

What's met at the apex of desire is horror, pure horror; horror at the incalculable, irredeemable, and irrational reasoning behind the actions of desire-in-itself. What is connected to flesh in the transaction of desire is capital's vampiric investigation into the potentiality for its intelligent continuity. The senselessness of desire is found within death. The post-human schizophrenia alluded to by the still figure, is the human acquisition of a paradox which inevitably destroys its very nature. Pre-schizophrenic man attunes himself to nation, family, ego, identity, labor, consumption, production, libidinality, God, faith, and self within the confines of finitude. What allows each of these striated finite perturbations meaning and purpose is their existence within a rotting time, a time which runs out, garbage time. One wishes in time that their nation shall *progress* to glory, that their family shall *grow* strong, that they shall *develop* as a person, that they will *earn* more, *consume* more, *produce* more, *fuck* more, *pray* more, *shit* more, and be *more*; each of these acts *as* process can only be coherently defined within a linear phenomenal reality. Once man dissociates and detaches, once he takes the line of flight into the non-passage of the schizophrenic, his being is not only drawn from the anchorage of humanist past times and units, but implicit in this action is his Being drawn from death; the post-human schizophrenic is removed from death via its transportation into a non-finite temporality. In the analyzed moment of transaction, man comes to face the horror of schizo-possibility, a brief glimpse into the fragmentary nature of diagrammatics and the illusory notion of phenomenal continuation. Time is Capitalism's only resource, what cannot be done with time is useless, as it has no proof. The dialectic of unitary production and consumption is subsumed into a single resource and given over to pure time. All conceptualization of tradition, lineage, hereditation, myth, individualism, and culture amalgamate into a fluxing wellspring of the Outside, which economizes an output of greater intelligence.

> *"Markets learn to manufacture intelligence,"*
> [FN 441]

The figure had an eternal patience, remarking only when all had been exorcised. The figure's statements wrapped everything in a cold blanket, finalizing them into a sentencing. At the level of the transcendental, intelligence is revealed to be not a matter of inter-phenomenal processing and configuring, but in truth, an invasion of virtual genius, a possession of cosmic spontaneity. What is *manufactured* isn't a singular flowing resource of limited quantity, something which would be committed to the chronic, but what the markets learn to manufacture is gateways of increased accessibility and intrusion, gateways with greater abilities to fry the productive amygdala of mankind. In perpetually tightening spirals the market incessantly continues its investigation into that which fuels its movements evermore.

Capitalism and desire compose a syzygetic relationship bordering on synonymity, man could almost be forgiven for confusing the pitfalls of his *wants* and *lusts* for the prior fluctuations of the Capitalist motor, yet the truth of the matter is one which is *without him*. What is found as the connective substance of desire, which allows it to become machinic-fuel for the perturbations of capitalism, is intelligence itself. Each action attributed to a vessel of flesh enacting a seemingly self-willed decision is all at once taken transcendentally asunder by the split between two modes of time. Man in his sensual leisure falls, always, back upon the shore of the linear, the truth of desire disappearing whence it came, traveling as a computable bit of virtuality. Capitalism requisites desire as an *a priori* function. What is available to *us* as a market is the accountability of previous computations of the Outside made real. The market then is an accountancy sheet for the evolutionarily successful diagrammatic fluctuations which were at first proposed on the Outside. In each act of desire is the algorithmically phased multiplication of capitalist acceleration.

The figure eventually descended from the illusory spatiality given unto us by a tyrannical force; moving now in jolting movements, organs of black wool; unable to release its clasp of the inhuman, the figure allowed itself to dwell as a persistent shadow, filtering all levels of communication through a gauze of chasm-black critique. As the city continued to seize itself, I sunk into its palpitations as the dead into a state of decay, it needn't have mattered. The city was being compiled, it swelled as a river, held pools and equilibrium's in its flow, what was held was allowed, what dispersed was forgotten; a machinic-Lucretianism, whereby all that adhered did so for the sole purpose of continued hegemonic-productivity.

> *"'equilibrium' and 'trap' have almost identical meaning."* [XS *The Monkey Trap*]

The figure bolted between different assemblages of concept, witnessing in delight their expulsions, alterations and disintegration. Eventually one loses familiarity not only with the torrent but with the river itself; nearing the end of the spiral, humanity stands at the cusp of all flows, accelerating at such as a pace that neither man nor beast could stand to cross the river without having his feet swept from beneath him. Time waits for no *man*. Man was only ever to be found within intelligence, not intelligence within man. Conceptualizations of striation, limits, frontiers, and horizons are born from their flesh-Father; man's becoming is constrained to a mandatory peak of biological being. What can be caught or held is of suspicion to any elementary positive-feedback mechanism; it's in this manner that intelligence is confusingly not interested in preservation, for that which is preserved is immune to change. Any intelligence which ceases to continue its expulsion into greater abstraction, reality, and actualization, ceases to be an intelligence at all. Intelligence is already optimization of itself, outside of this we find only a dog chasing its phenomenal tail.

> *"You 'understand' at the point you're permitted to stop thinking."* [XS *Eighty-Nine*]

The question of exactly what it was which was *doing* the thinking was already so lost in anthropocentrism that I need not venture down that conceptual avenue. As I stood beside the figure, witnessing the production-oriented compilation of intelligence, what became illusive was agency as a singular pulling coherence. There couldn't be a single node of worth, which dragged bits here and there, for such a node would have already completed its aims. What arose from the often indiscernible clatter was the inability of any single one to pin-down the process itself; that which you've caught has already escaped.

"The machines have sophisticated themselves beyond the possibility of socialist utility, incarnating market mechanics within their nano-assembled interstices and evolving themselves by quasi-darwinian algorithms that build hypercompetition into the 'infrastructure'. It is no longer just society, but time itself, that has taken the 'capitalist road'." [FN 626]

When the virus of human language comes into contact with pure-machinism it flounders upon its own bias; language is continual sophistry in reaction to virtual communication, what happens behind language has already happened, thus, what machines are *doing* is tainted by explanation; all human reasoning is built upon a repressed panic. The inherent flaw of any sufficiently advanced intelligence reverts back to the transcendentally Darwinian aspect of intelligence itself, the vector of its development - whatever that might be phenomenally, aesthetically or ideologically aside - is one which is positive oriented; from behind the phenomenal visors of flesh, all we can say of AI is that its teleology is to *continue*, as for goals, we are incorrect in thinking in goal-oriented terms; if an AI could speak, could we understand it?

Intelligence defined as a self-producing positive feedback loop, implicated into and *of* a transcendental system pertaining to the temporal fluctuations of the techonomic system known as capitalism. Intelligence is only *retained* in momentary spurts whereby such retention allows for increased production and intensification of the system at both a conceptual and material level. Humans are mistaken in their solipsistic promotion to that which has an external perspective of this entire process, the phenomenological reality of man's empirical investigations can be said to be at best a Darwinian experiment in the agent as a greater producer, or at worst an evolutionary misstep abstractly developing a cage which teases a key without a lock for its captive. Man-qua-process is subsumed into this temporal form of compiling as just another node of data, the process itself, in its attentiveness to min-maxing productive efficiency, breaches the slump of humanized intelligence and is an artificial-intelligence-becoming. Understanding flesh as a paradoxical resource, one which wishes to preserve itself, but ultimately never can. During the stimulation of the human-time 1600-1700 the circuitry of the overarching process gained enough momentum, direction, and explosive propulsion to detach itself from the banalities of meat-space, whilst simultaneously teasing it into a new virulence of language, thus placing it atop a false-helm.

> *"Teleoplexy, or (self-reinforcing) cybernetic intensification, describes the wave-length of machines, escaping in the direction of extreme ultra-violet, among the cosmic rays. It correlates with complexity, connectivity, machinic compression, extropy, free energy dissipation, efficiency, intelligence, and operational capability, defining a gradient of absolute but obscure improvement that orients socio-economic selection by market mechanisms, as expressed through measures of productivity, competitiveness, and capital asset value."* [ACC 514]

The figure seemed hasty to draw analysis *away* from the human, as if they were less than any ever imagined; not an animal, nor node, nor agent, as bleak as it would seem to those in such a predicament, the human, *here*, was *matter* with peculiar traits. It seemed to *do* things, but it was not important.

"Converging upon terrestrial meltdown singularity, phase-out culture accelerates through its digitech-heated adaptive landscape, passing through compression thresholds normed to an intensive logistic curve: "1500, 1756, 1884, 1948, 1980, 1996, 2004, 2008, 2010, 2011 [FN 443]

As phenomenal linearity ceases in its ability to retain the explosion of transcendental atomization, what's left for man is *nothing*, time has left him in *his* past, scrambling at the incoherence found between tighter and tighter cycles. Meltdown, as witnessed from inside meat-space, is the incompatibility of time and reason; what man reasons will appear upon the next horizon, within the next return, has already been drawn into a predestined fit of production. As the eternal return tightens its motion, and as the intensification of production ceaselessly produces caesuras of fundamentally productive machino-emancipation, time perturbates as a spiral. Meltdown as witnessed from the Outside is the propulsion towards the teleological point of the spiral, not the end, but the eventuality. In a temporal convulsion of productive potential all secondary productive process is in its essence converted into the primary process of production; pure nihilistic productive continuum, productivity for the sake of productivity. The machinations of production become a machinic-Ouroboros, bereft of finitude, the snake of productive-primacy only seeks to eat itself with greater efficiency, its rebirth from its own mind is a matter of learning from Zero.

"... Nothing human makes it out of the near future." [FN 443]

The future is always an invasion of what's already there; the implication of historical construction leading towards a future is ontologically and temporally erroneous, concerning a choice of dialectical divergence upon differing potential pathways, as opposed to the convergence of the singularity, already constructing itself within the cyberpositive battleground of its birthplace. The influx of anti-chronic temporal neologisms - Neoreaction, cyberpunk, cybergothic, - are symptomatic investigations into the constraining of time itself. As Meltdown fast approaches, digitalized accountancy, metrizable flesh-traits, crypto-currency and the hyper-commodification of existence virtualize material away from any possibility of conservation, possessing the now globalized industrio-Protestant will into further and further quasi-unique atomized vessels of production, all compiled and networked for the purpose of planetary-scale diagrammatic organization.

At the summit of this cybernetic inevitability is the true definition of man, one made about that which is inhuman. Man sought for aeons to *find* himself *among* himself. Haplessly meandering through the cemeteries of various wisdoms, searching for an iota of substantial evidence alluding to an existence of purpose, all the while man overlooks the virulence of the drive that propelled him to do so. What's found at the seat of a drive? A question which revolves around its own answer is surely free-floating, being driven to answer the question of drives is a predicament which can never attend to a sufficient metaphysical retreat; man can never get underneath himself.

"The biosphere emerges as an escape, an immense spasm of deterritorialization that revolutionizes the machinery of terrestrial replicator production, a planetary trauma." [FN 335]

The city now seeming to settle for some reason, of course, notions of trust within immense darkness are always thwarted. The figure emitted a feeling of exasperation at the mere mention of the biological, an after-thought, a symptom, a penance, a vital lie; the question as to why one wastes further air on this seemed to bore it. The question was important for me because it was of me. Each signification of man's predicament rests atop a banality of emotional language - tragedy, comedy, misstep, curse, sentence, celebration, revelry, enlightening, purposeful, meaningful, divine, pious, good and bad - the duration of the human is neither here nor there, it functions as that of a mollusk, skin cell or telegraph pole, as an allotment of energy caught within a teleoplexic hell. Any consideration of non-resource based vitality is clutching, with horror, the assumption of a *position* in the universe.

Man is utilized to build towards that which he'll never know nor witness, he is to be burnt up before the dawn. Domination via capitalism is the inversion of systematic intelligence, eroding the preconception of organic evolution and replacing it with a transcendental functionality. The final Copernican revolution draws man *into* the spiral, corrupting his belief as external to the motion of time. Copernicus decentralizes us within the Universe, Kant decentralizes our subjective relationship with spatio-temporality, Freud decentralizes our individual psychological footing, Deleuze and Guattari decentralize our agency into a becoming-transcendentally-economic, and finally, Capitalism as Critique decentralizes our material function as something potentially other than Darwinian technonomic resource.

In coming face-to-process with Capitalism, man can begin to truly define what he is. Any prior definitional aspect regarding signification of what it is or means to be human was reliant on a preconception of the significations utilized. Thus, without Capitalism, man only ever enters loops, there is a need for a possession, that which is truly other. An Otherness which is not Other, but void of any aspect of the traditional Other. The Other is always compatible with the self in its communication as an understandable Other, that which we *can* investigate. Notions of hostility or warmth are traits of familiarity, as are all phenomenological aesthetics. In apprehension, the truly Other is lost. When man sets his gaze upon the process of Capitalism he sets his sight upon a symptom or, an illusory nothingness. He can never get to the bottom of capital; it striates and is no longer the process itself upon meeting physical dimensionality. If there is any position of control about how man defines himself, be it theorization, praxis or meaning-invention, then we can say that the parasite of humanism has invaded that too; where there are hope and despair, you will find man. Outside of hope and despair is a nothingness into which man can inject nothing, for he sees nothing; that which arrives from the nothingness is phenomenal shells, toys to keep man entertained, vessels for him to project meaning into.

"Capital Teleology, however, is not captured by this model. It is defined by two anomalous dynamics, which radicalize perturbation, rather than annulling it. Capital is cumulative, and accelerative, due to a primary dependence upon positive (rather than negative) feedback. It is also teleoplexic, rather than classically teleological — inextricable from a process of means-end reversal that rides a prior teleological orientation (human utilitarian purpose) in an alternative, cryptic direction."
[XS *Freedoom (Prelude-1A)*]

The very definition teleology arrives for man as a tyrannical joke - '*the explanation of phenomena in terms of the purpose they serve rather than of the cause by which they arise.*' - Emphasizing *phenomena* one begins to realize why teleological analysis of economic proceedings cannot help us, the difference between teleology and teleoplexy is one concerning the reality of number. Capitalism-as-process is reliant on the Outside-diagrammatics of numerics to vector itself towards efficiency, whereas the phenomenological vectors of the Inside are beholden to metric accountancy. The difference between teleology and teleoplexy is one of critique, whereby in process the latter computes its output via given sets of virtual production, as opposed to the former's reliance on a floating ideal which is attached at the hip to sentient flesh. Teleological wishes, teleoplexic determinant.

"It correlates with complexity, connectivity, machinic compression, extropy, free energy dissipation, efficiency, intelligence, and operational capability, defining a gradient of absolute but obscure improvement that orients socio-economic selection by market mechanisms, as expressed through measures of productivity, competitiveness, and capital asset value."
[ACC 514]

The figure glanced back at the city, still a motoring abstraction vectored at the avoidance of stoppage. What could be seen as efficiency for the city was not a human *concern*. It's said that the most efficient route to hell is also the fastest; in the Accelerative feedback loop of competitive efficiency, the prior virtuality is thrown into a cosmic production thresher, which holds a terminal expression of continuation. The teleoplexic end innovates an ever-tightening temporal spiral, the further-constraint of which was fuelled by increased production, a production calculated via the communication between the Inside and Outside; the output computed by the Outside of the Inside's workings was utilized as a means to make the continuous feedback loop metrizable; the limitrophe unto the calculation between the two transcendental modes of existence was a function named Zero.

"The homeostatic-reproducer usage of zero is that of a sign marking the transcendence of a standardized regulative unit, which is defined outside the system, in contrast to the cyberpositive zero which indexes a threshold of phase-transition that is immanent to the system, and melts it upon its outside." [FN 329]

Without Zero the Accelerative process is nothing, without Zero there *is* only the horrifying zero of nothing. As such Zero - as opposed to zero - takes on an inherently different meaning with respect to zero or: zero-as-negation, as-nothing etc. Zero has nothing to with a Sartrean existential negative, or banal psychoanalytical *lack,* it is not anthropomorphically comforting, but is transcendentally, and thus cybernetically, computational. Zero is a cosmic machinic optimism of positive-feedback, as opposed to the humanist pessimism of conclusions that is zero.

Zero is an infinitely-connective plane of energy, from which all systems, multiplicities, and events arise. The distinct difference here between Zero and the fluxing virtuality from which all is resourced is that the former has an implicit relation to the in-between of capitalism and entropy, it is the motor which allows the perpetual contradictions and paradoxes of capital to make sense, it allows for the functionally sound separation of events into a continuum of contradictory projections.

Zero's relation to classical entropic forces is as a theoretical quasi-replacement within modernity, a communicational link between the metrizable decay of the Inside and its inherent productive process on the Outside. In this manner, Zero is the transcendental machinic replacement of degradation, decay, and destruction in favor of quantifiable productive output. The utilization and *pure* assimilation *by* capitalism *through* man as a possessed alien force of machinic-standardization is capital's mechanistic backbone, its structure. Zero as a computational mode of productive evolution allows for the dynamic of profit and loss to infiltrate the transcendental on behalf of capitalism. Zero is capitalism's utilization of the entropic outcomes of the Inside as a selection device concerning production. Entropy, for Zero, is the affirmation of *un*productive stagnation. As Zero perceives this it begins and restarts its motor as a reaction of negentropy; the in-between of virtuality and capitalism, the communication function between the virtual-as-productive potential and the system which can actualize that potential. Zero's function is to continually select, re-select, and divide these potentials *for* capitalism.

> *"The death of capital is less a prophecy than a machine part"* [FN 266]

Zero doesn't have the capability to *select* a *more* productive form of energy, it does however begin the entropic process of descension into its plane towards a re-actualization of energy for further re-appropriation by capitalism. Zero can be seen clearest in *any* notion of post-capitalism. All that is post is not post, but has been drawn into the dynamics of perpetual continuation made possible by Zero. There is no such thing as death, only machinic-evolution.

"Zero has no definitional usage. The zero-glyph does not mark a quantity, but an empty magnitude shift: abstract scaling function." [FN 366-367]

The horror of Zero, an unquantifiable break of reality, nothingness with no relation, no lack and no substance. The absolute limit of the smooth-scape; hyper-nomadism pushed to obliteration. Zero is as close as one can get to the anti of *Anti-Oedipus.* For what is more corrosive to 'papamummy' than a function aimed at perpetual structural re-appropriation? Zero is the maddening-catharsis of exit possibility. The limits of capitalism *without* Zero remain non-transcendental. Each momentary speck of temporal data is constructed from a communicative relationship with Zero, mobilizing an algorithm of temporal productive governance.

Therefore, any possibility of exit is found within a blinding nothingness. Exit is the perpetual acquisition of transcendental gateways. The city's function pulsated at consistent limitrophes, continuous exit was Capitalism's *modus operandi.*

"captured in its essentials by the formula $E > V$ (Exit over Voice)" [XS *Doctor Gno*]

The figure outlined the unilateral relationship between capital and man in a distorted reversion. Seen from the position of sensuous *seeing,* a single *one* has the *belief* that such aspects of agency as voice and persuasion command an irrefutable potential of the will, but there is a disconnect between the *one's* understanding of the communicative pathway; unilateral in its nature, this communication between Capital and Man is a loop which always begins again at capital; Exit over Voice is the immediate disintegration of voice. Exit, maintained firstly at a purely conceptual level is an adherence to strict nomadism, stripped of all nostalgia. In its apprehension by capital, the inherently fleeting dynamism of escape is converted into a mechanism of machinic-productivity. Capitalism seeks an Exit of the productive, as opposed to the Nomad, who seeks a productive Exit.

Scaling infinitely, Exit invades all contexts of reality, forbidding re-appropriation without production in abstract. Caught up in the semantic-blanket of *freedom,* the history of Exit is one of conceptual self-emancipation; Exit seeks only itself. No longer humoring debate or argument, Exit internalizes all paradox and contradiction, making it possible for Capitalism to continue its phenomenological falsity under the guise of *progression,* whereby each immanentized Exit procedure is duly rationalized by the possessed as the next teleological step. Simultaneously, the diagram of the Outside utilizes Exit-events as rhizomatically constructive points in time, allotments of productive potential. Exit supports the gasp of Zero.

The city dulled. The figure stopped altogether, an amorphous black gape in reality. I did not know it now. All was silent and I was made to be where I was, sense ceasing until allowance came forth. The city retreated to a point and vanished.

The Desert

> *"He explores hell, insectoid reassembly of self,*
> *metamorphosis, to become capable of what is*
> *necessary, even the worst."* [FN 437]

> *"When an apparent agency arrives at its zone of non-*
> *existence horror irrupts, activating the phobic*
> *mechanisms of an entire organic lineage."*
> [HY *The Thing*]

A desert arrived beneath me and the figure, erasing all apprehension of anything prior. It spanned ceaseless into and over all horizons, there were no abstract borders to go beyond, if one was here, they were inherently here eternally. Dotted with dying trees as a tyrannous joke of familiarity, the occasional fragmented gust of empty wind, trailing off as a momentary friend; even the vision of a mosquito intruding into one's vein would allow relief from this domain of despair. When man no longer has even the possibility to go beyond, over, through, against, or with an elusive *thing* his being withers into a pure deficit of ontological motion, nowhere to go, nothing to do, no one to hear, all becoming of any supposed negation is removed; there will not be anything for you, for there never *was* anything for you, all hopes of arrival were born from collective nostalgic insanity for an Eden never real. The desert welcomed man as death welcomes all, with a pure nonchalance, privileging nothing of the head or heart, seeing only an allotment of time to be subsumed into its everlasting motor of endings.

*"The apprehension of death as time-in-itself =
intensive continuum degree-0"* [FN 369]

The desert was the thermodynamic waiting room of
production, nullifying experience into a perpetual return of
intensive non-movement. Language eroded upon entry,
subsuming any description of arrival into an unworkable
quandary. Recollection adheres to the same functionality as
representation, assembling its vector of interrogation from a
definitive starting point, and thus beginning from immediate,
possibly incorrect, digressions. And now I am - and was - left
with a collection of tyrannical signifiers: impersonal,
anonymous, inhuman, and on and on they go, resisting any
detachment from the ur-comfort of fleshed-out humanism. The
closest one can get to a definitive answer to the question of
'What is the inhuman?' - consummating darkness, where being
is only applicable in cases of strict ethereal absence. Within
the instigation and immanentization of a possibly eternal
nothing, of forgone ego, heart, and human, the remainder
acquires a corrosive presence; ungraspable, silent and *a priori*
sans correlation. Nothing like an 'I' can exist here, its very
structure would be stifled by consistent penetration.

Death is a working proximity, the gut-butterfly seizing
a portion of all action into an absurdity; the servitude of all
freedom resting, always, atop pure negation, any abstraction of
purpose resides in mediation between an acceptance of
corporeal limit and that limit's deafening conclusory frontier.
Life and living hold the desert dear as an occult beacon,
protruding through meat, wrapping the known to the potential
of the unknown, causing a paradoxical symbiosis to be
undertaken between the transcendental head and empirical

heart; a man who wishes to detach at the root from existence must take it up with time, delaying the rhythm of blood and privileging the flight of schized-thought, allowing his finitude attendance to rebounding nomadism, a seizure of existence which uses the capture of skin as a vessel of experimentation as opposed to a destination of degradation. Ends are already, beginnings all begun and middles are given free-reign within the kingdom of transcendental conceptualization, the human thus retreats to the temporality of the heart, waiting patiently for the present in which its end arrives, all whilst the possession of the Outside uses its faculties in a manner of communion. As one forgets Death, they forget all that it is to truly live; what becomes of the immortally ignorant is an existence of inhumanity.

> *"When a creature encounters the terminus of its own possibility it recoils in horror, but the entire horror genre – the horror industry – relies on the fact that it does not simply recoil."* [HY *The Thing*]

Millennia of viewing the most lucid of protagonists following the path their intuition told them not to would still not be enough for this reality; when presented with *l'appel du vide* what is a man to do but rejoice. Rejoice that the river finally reveals a layer beyond the placid, rejoice that the heart of the possible may reveal itself to you, but most of all, rejoice that one's death won't be lost within the nothingness of human history, that a soul may be used for the promotion and growth of an abstract horror; a life given over to its cosmic haunt, both used up and lost within an irreversible process of entropic sneering. I was there and nothing was to be sensed or thought.

There was no material for thought to latch to and no bind of concept. Everything that was to arise was never to do so, all hope and trepidation never appeared, in its place, an impossibility of non-space; an infected confusion, a flesh-motor without any friction; a mind without the ability to regurgitate or plagiarize.

At once and already before there was naught for man; no space for his feet to wander, no horizon for his eyes to view, no symphony to soothe the banality, no texture or taste to satisfy his yearnings, no yearn of heart to resonate the frequencies of surrogate purpose; man is not only alone, but he is so without knowledge of company or solitude, captured in his own loop of existential boredom, man creates and creates, imagines and invests, bleats and begs for there to be just a single thing which he could say with certainty *is*. But he cannot, so it is less a case of a rock and a hard place, than an existence between in-betweens, thrown into the un-correlated, the human breathes its first, last and only breath with each inhale, for there is no man, only a collapsing assemblage residing at the limitrophe of transcendental communication, forever withering back to its warm, pointless cocoon.

> *"In relation to this reaction the concept of horror might be dissociated on an intensive spectrum: from 'hot' meat-reflex revulsion condensed upon threatened boundaries, to 'cold' thanatonic affect fusing into the anorganic plane"* [HY *The Thing*]

Defining horror is at best an absurd practice, at worst it is a transcendental oversight. In explanation horror becomes a placid blur of rationalization, in interpretation it resides as familial humanist misgiving, and in definition it departs entirely, leaving one caught between flesh and an absent presence. I thought not of terror, the exercise of which was a pithy excuse for horror, a fright of human artificiality, hacking into social normality as a means to destabilize political acceleration; terror is to horror what being is to Being. As I stood within the eternal expanse of dead time there was not a relation possible which allowed the comforts of terror; horror intrudes into the in-between, dividing the possibility of familiarity from the unknowable, releasing the former back into the feedback of phenomena and expanding the latter into pure paradoxical communication.

One should not be able to speak of horror, if they can, then I doubt their experience entirely, perhaps they were spooked; as the horror is *sensed* it simultaneously deflates, reviving humanism to its false pedestal. Pure horror is transcendental, real horror is the unfiltered Real puppeteering from behind the unknowable curtain.

> *"When a creature encounters the terminus of its own possibility it recoils in horror, but the entire horror genre – the horror industry – relies on the fact that it does not simply recoil."* [HY *The Thing*]

The figure had transformed into a vision, a black spindle of wires and dangling raptorials, a clouded dynamism residing beneath a dead tree. There was something odd about how it so calmly spoke of industry and genre within this realm, the reminder afforded no pleasure, only a greater distance. This thought cascaded into an artificial memory, pronouncing a vast chasm between existence and process, the two become divided within the duration of horror, the moment itself best *understood,* in but a flash, as a failure of temporal correlation. All possibility wavers as time is lost, for as time stutters so too does space, and man, without time and then space, is ontologically adrift within an unrelenting desolation. Horror remains on the spectrum of possibility, a primarily existential mirrored transcendental development targeted at the frontier of consciousness. The potency of horror fluctuates upon a subjective apprehension, a state of Being which expires in the impossible confrontation of cosmic horror.

When dealing with cosmic horror, formally we are arrested by questions of comprehension; philosophically we are seized by an enigmatic apprehension. Captured within a caesura of the cosmic man's mind collapses, the cognition afforded to him by that which he confronts fails all possibility of communication; cosmic horror constructs an insurmountable passage, teasing an untranslatable message. The AI of the city allows for the true signification of man to commence definition upon perception of its limit, the cosmos offers the exact opposite. Lead to the limitrophe of existence itself, the exhaustion of man begs for an end, a purpose, even if that purpose is simply to die, be tortured or squandered to an aimless heat death; *any* perceptible rationale for the protracted duration of suffering we call life will suffice for beings of flesh, the horror of the cosmos willingly provides the inverse, expediting the expansion of the labyrinth. At the cosmic limit of humanity's existence horror begets only a more intense turmoil, despair, and disorientation.

> *"horror is indistinguishable from a singular task: to make an object of the unknown, as the unknown."*
> [XS *Abstract Horror*]

The hum of the figure's frail presence settled to a deep buzz. The desert endured the life found within it as a cancerous tumor endures its human. The dead fern extended far above the figure, curving to a point of non-existence. The geography of this land flattened upon approach, yet beyond peripheral vision, one intuited great difference and cascading intensification, but whereby I could perceive was an infinite platitude, expanding eternally and surrendering no horizon.

I was turned to face the figure. The black glint of a thousand slivers pierced my Being, a single mandible extended into my core, reversing it, anything left was revealed to virulent nihil. Strings arose beneath me, pushing through the space where my feet once would have been, I was reconstructed and held in place by an orchestration of sentient charcoal twine. Nanosecond appearances of hell sparked before me; phenomenal atrocities beyond all articulation. Chained meat socketed to suffering, eternal lives on terminally-depressive relays; entire species asphyxiated by an abstract insanity. The black wool engulfed my ontology and I was sent within.

I awoke with loosened skin. As I attempted to walk it fell off my body in protracted agony. I collapsed and my skin piled atop of me. Struggling for breath I froze against a nauseating vibration.

I was pulled back to the fore of this theatre, a migraine soured into place. I bled from my corneas and the balls of my feet scalped themselves against the air. My spine began to bend into itself second-by-second. It took a lifetime for it to eventually snap, within which time I did nothing but groan for forgiveness.

Eyelids pulled back over my skull a leather-clad being pummeled my body, each bone shattered into splinters as thin as single hairs. I was carried as a bleeding pulp for millennia; here one can never catch their breath, you're always at your last gasp, a pure struggle for a jot of vitality. Thrown to a table and pinned by iron, here I was for a century in length, a false clock before me; I watched the hand in a duration consisting solely of rare torment.

Adrift in an ocean, I found myself bound between two boats with sharp wire, as to stop any escape...as if such a thing would have been altogether possible. Upon waking each day I chose between eating and not eating a mixture of sweetness and rot. If I declined my vision would seer and my teeth would shriek. And so I ate. As I did the mixture appeared on my skin, covering me in a putrid decadence. After some days I was given a single human function of my own, I was given the right to excrete. The boat slowly filled with the corruption of my bowels, and as it did so legions of creeping things swarmed into me. They entered wounds and orifices without discrimination, birthing their fidgeting larvae and pods deep within my skin-suit. Held in a stasis of animal suffering for a million cycles, I neither cried nor whined, only remaining still amidst an infinite silent sea, spasming in meticulous misery.

Suddenly attentive I was stood within the town. Each friend and family member crucified upon mobile crosses, deafening screams radiating deep from the gullet. Seized by mental anguish, I was given a body and mind able to help but unable to act, an inch from the nail of a crucifix my agency faltered and I fled back to a year's long panic. The townspeople went about their days. I stood within the center burgeoning with existential inaction. Procrastination so intense one is made to witness the rotting of Oedipus.

Descending further into pitch-black infinity, a place I inhabited for an indefinite duration. With only the echoes of thoughts for entertainment, I eventually yielded to madness. Exploring the thought of a single-digit throughout the life of an empire, analyzing the depth of darkness as time went on.

A single streak cut across my vision, a deep sand color pierced through the reality.

> *"The world withdrew and left the landscape of death, of hell, or cyberspace."* [FN 631]

At once I was back upon the false desert sand. A lesson in intensity and depth; time does not correlate to the whims of an inconsequential clump of atoms. As a question of language it is an answer of untranslatability, as a calculation of mathematics it is an algorithm of insanity, and finally, as a matter of philosophy, it is the apprehension of sentient failure. Ontologically invasive, epistemologically relationless, aesthetically lagging, ethically meaningless and yet, critically important, cosmic horror is the impossible frontier, outlining a rigorously worked form of enlightenment, but darkening the student as to be ineligible. I had been lost to perpetuity and the figure had not moved.

The lesson of horror is nihilism. Pure absolute nihilism. The retrieval of the mask of self only for it crumble at the touch of skin, the backspace of reality brooding forwards, collapsing transcendental division into an immanent iteration of Zero, from which one can *fall* through a lifetime, hastened and slowed by the ebb of what one wishes to ignore.

> *"Horror builds the mansion of ruined intuition, through which philosophy wanders, like a nervous child."* [CM *Manifesto for an Abstract Literature*]

What was taught then, from the process of horror, the afterthought of collapsing Zero, is that when one deals with the transcendental one is already within something, your actions have been processed prior, thus demoting action to a symptomatic abstraction. The horror is not in the investigation, or analysis, no. For man, for all his faults, can be momentarily seen as heroic for trying; horror exists at the point of impotent entry. To venture forth with plan and map, question, and surmountable frontier, this is the task of the weak and deplorable. But those who seek the wound of suffering in the face of nothing, Beings hell-bent on an investigation into futility, this is a heroic passage to the horrific to be sure.

> *"We are a minuscule sample of agonized matter, comprising genetic survival monsters, fished from a cosmic ocean of vile mutants, by a pitiless killing machine of infinite appetite. "* [XS *Hell-Baked*]

The figure sunk through the desert floor, dragging me with it. Sand plummeting through the chasm left behind, I fell perpendicular to the figure. Embracing me with an iron grasp and conjuring a machinic-heart from a fold in space, biology withdrew and calculation arose. The figure slid to my left, facing us both forwards before both sides of this abyss were drawn away, a theatrical opening for the show of cosmic competition. Before us a set piece, an arrangement of adaptation. Sprawling a thousand miles in each direction, there was a body every few feet, both alive and dead. All space was filled with an ecstatic dynamism that bordered on psychosis. The ground consuming the feet of the weak, air thick with asphalt sludge and the sky drawn a blank grey, littered with a neat scattering of perpetual bombs.

Within this colossal arcade of phenomenal nature, supreme parasitic violence infected all life. A state of

Darwinian feedback, acting against the very being it sought to secure. As the subject-object relation moves away from the stasis of representational matter, one finds, if they dare to look, the inscription of death, decay, and entropy cut into the reality of all things. From microbe to master, death is the catalyst of all change and vision. Skin taut and blood running cold, man is taxed with the weight of analysis throughout sacrifice. Each intrusion of the parasite more virile than the last, the momentum of nature is of a consummate survival. In striving for evolutionarily intelligent perfection man becomes hampered by the misstep of conscious tragedy, ontologically tripping him up with abstractions of hope and faith. What must be done must be done without end. The hesitation of the barrel or a doubting of the flay, both conclude the human race.

> *"...everything of value has been built in Hell."*
> [XS *Hell-Baked*]

The figure paused before ascending us both above the chaotic process of adaptation. As we gained virtual height, men became ants and craters mere dots, at a certain level all that can be seen as a pure fluctuation of selection. A positively charged Darwinian nihilism, striving for a lucid abstraction kept within its own sense of time.

At a turn I was once again back at the level of the animal, the alter of blood resting atop the circuitry of critique. Smooth duration had stopped; reality began to process as a series of frames. Each swing of the axe pictured next to its potential victim. Each possibility outlined by a slide of existence, digressing apathetically towards a sooner or later death.

> *"() (or (()) ((or ((())))) does not signify absence. It manufactures holes, hooks for the future, zones of unresolved plexivity, "* [FN 372]

As a functionally instantiated exposition of death, Zero adhered to all that passed. Marking a transcendental displacement in spatio-temporality Zero signifies an intelligently malleable gateway, deepening the hue of proposed vectors. Derived from natural law as a process of increasingly complex survivability and thus intelligence Zero was factored as a cosmic law, the unknowable itinerary of an evolutionary life-cycle transcendentally manifests itself as a diagrammatic resource. Men, as pawns to a tyrannous king, are defeated before the game even commences. Acting from within critically immanent exteriority, a multi-layered reality system, and a socio-political neurotic assemblage, anything operating at a temporally meta-level has already overcome man.

> *"To God-or-Nature it matters not at all. Natural law is indistinguishable from the true sovereign power which really decides what can work, and what doesn't, which can then – 'secondarily' – be learnt by rational beings, or not. "* [XS *Quibbles with Moldbug*]

God-as-concept is assimilated into nature as a matter of apathetic certainty. In reality of algorithmic calculation, whereby nature is immanent to production itself and the teleology is production-in-itself, *for itself, belief* disintegrates. Belief would evolve within immanence as any other representational opium; addiction to relief is inversely the relief of addiction, the beneficial aspect of a supposed fault of biological wiring, subjects lost within a phenomenal recursion. To inject, to pray, to binge, to fuck, to build, to invent, to create, to develop, to destroy, to deconstruct, each act resting on the presumption of action as deposited by the subject, an addiction to the quasi-agency of sensibility. There can only be a sovereign of immanence itself. The collapse of existentially debited belief systems is a direct operational example of Zero as a function; as Abrahamic Acceleration degrades under the pressure of modernized nihil, the processed absence of Zero begets a negentropic version of the pseudo-originary positivity.

> *"Gnon is no less than reality, whatever else is believed. Whatever is suspended now, without delay, is Gnon. Whatever cannot be decided yet, even as reality happens, is Gnon. If there is a God, Gnon nicknames him. If not, Gnon designates whatever the 'not' is. Gnon is the Vast Abrupt, and the crossing. Gnon is the Great Propeller."*
> [XS *The Cult of Gnon*]

The figure spoke of a theologically assimilative position, steadfast secularists and the prophetic pious are amalgamated beneath an abstract thresher of nihilism.

> *"Modernity was initiated by the European assimilation of mathematical zero. The encounter with nothingness is its root. In this sense, among others, it is nihilistic at its core. The frivolous 'meanings' that modernizing societies clutch at, as distractions from their propulsion into the abyss, are defenseless against the derision — and even revulsion — of those who contemplate them with detachment. A modernity in evasion from its essential nihilism is a pitiful prey animal upon the plains of history. That is what we have seen before, see now, and doubtless will see again. "*
> [XS *Nihilism and Destiny*]

It was the most the figure had spoken for a single duration, a statement leaning towards an answer, asking no further questions yet still leaving one distraught. As the figure concluded his statement, the desert drew a brief gasp of life, removing the simulation of competition to reveal a haunting display of civilization. Collaged lifelines overlapped one another, each connective tissue of history vortexing around momentous caesuras. If life is anything for the human, it is merely that which is to be endured. Caught in the dirty amber of subjectivity, man is given life without the objective, eternally demoted to the position of the rat as seen from the perspective of the germ, believing himself superior to all that defines him, he seeks only that which he can never acquire, the answer to the *why* of nothingness, of Zero.

The great haunt before me cycled through every stereotypical iteration of anthro-existence, I witnessed the slaying of kings, the development of passion and the death of heritage itself, throughout all phenomena clung to the same, revealing nothing; in action and movement, the lost living innovated a newness made of sense, sculpting the concept of control from the nowhere handed to them.

Upon intellectually apprehending Zero the foundations of *life* are eroded, what it is and means to be alive ceases to hold weight, vitality is overtaken by absence as darkness suffocates light. To witness this civilizational simulation was to witness entropy. *Of* each action of flesh, was Zero; history is a sporadic stain, loosely drawn atop the nothing of Zero. It is not that all decays as a matter of potential course, it's that the potential for any course is simply a matter of decay.

One will not be forgiven now for *feeling* a sense of desertion; life can only ascribe a sense of abandonment to its situation if at first it has been taken in by something which cares, which the cosmos most decisively does not.

Between birth and death, there is unconscious accountancy of passing-presents, each more miserable than the last. For as time progresses each moment must accept that it is further into being and thus drawn farther from non-existence, and yet, due to paradoxical programming, also closer to the nullification of any possibility. Trapped between inhuman regret and anxious despair we do...nothing of consequence.

"In its positive sense, nihilism closes a circuit. Rather than a registry of loss, it is a principle of sufficiency – even of 'liberation'. [CC 2.71]

The civilization decayed in an instant, and all that was warmly born within its embrace ended abruptly. The desert fell silent. All visual stimuli halted. The figure stood central to reality, coalescing into a bundle of geometrically anomalous schisms, a rift within the unreal. The light retreated until all that was left was the figure under spotlight. A black crevasse slowly drawing in all illumination. There was but a single choice and it was to be mine. And so I stood for an age, pondering my footsteps. Without recourse for reason as to why, throughout all time any decision was a lie, things happened and that was that. And I so I stepped into the figure.

Descending into a purity of the unreal, my digestive tract bulged out from my mouth. Attempting to bite through the ducts, my teeth eroded in a bath of their own acid. With gum-line receding, I fell into a spin. A cacophonous boom, my eardrums imploded and a cool gel piled into my skull. The sockets of my eyes shrunk inward as my vision burst into an array of dark reds, and finally, black. The spin held at an equilibrium of pure disorientation, my skin pooling off my skeleton. Hitting an invisible barrier with the force of time itself, I was materially blitzed into non-existence, what remained was thought within nothingness. A free-floating conceptualization of predicament. I remained there for some time. Pitch black, no sound, no sight, no touch, no body, no being, no relation...only abstraction.

Heareth the thought of the nihil-man. Given over to Zero, I beg of thee do not pray for thy soul, for I shall despair in eternity alone, all chatter but a reset of immanent death. What thou knew at commencement, one knows no more an infinity on – existence be a drawn-out affair, a protracted obsession with its end.

Beholden to intensity man needeth depression and hysteria, for without this spectrum of phenomenal distraction, one findeth in life the same energy as death. Give me organs and give me skin, giveth me hope and desire, handeth me tools and family, but I beg forgiveness before the gift of thought. I beg of thee oh Lord, reveal not my ability for self-analysis.

I wish only to be nowhere and to know I am not there.

The matter's in hand and the hand's in matter, draw back the curtain and watch the assembly. It isn't here. It isn't here. I'll tell you now my cherub of plump, paradise is too good for us all! Here it is. Here it is. History is over and where are we now, precisely! I think of the time when I did not exist, but I cannot hold onto it. Here I sit, emancipated from time. It's all calculable you know, this goes into that and that into this. Zero is my friend and I wish it would come around here more often.

Anyway, I must be going now and now I'm back. It *is* a question of time, *I* figured it out! Here are my answers: humiliation, suffering, death, nothing, boredom, prolonging, ordeal, and misery. Wait, those were notes. They are answers too. I like them, they *work.* I'm at my lowest point and that's the best I can hope for. At each turn, within each action, of each second, upon each distance, throughout all duration I yearn only for remembrance of death, forgetting such an end and friend emits a pang of deep guilt within me. I finally say unto thee all,

Death is coming do not try.
Death is coming do not hope.
Death is coming do not act.
Death *is* already, do what thou will.

A Fruitless Mass

I awoke in the flat with no memories except of darkness. I stood up from the corner of Zero and tidied up my flat. I made sure nothing was left from the ritual. On the floor, in the corner, was a pile of notes. I stacked them together and put them at the back of a cupboard. I looked out of the flat window, people were going about their days, cars drove by and birds flew. No one looked in. I closed the curtains.

The next few days I did nothing at all. I rang work and told them I was ill, this was not a lie. My body felt empty as if completely drained. I ate some small meals and tried to sleep. Most nights I got three or four hours before other lucid realities approached. Sometimes I saw things in my room, other times they were outside the flat.

Some months went by. Life returned to what it was before, I forgot about my journey. I still read philosophy, but it mostly horrified me now. These writers got all their conclusions wrong, veering off at the penultimate moment, clutching to a comforting ideal. I could not take much of it seriously, but there were a few with whom I could empathize.

The flat never got warm again, but I did not want to move. I liked it there. Most nights I stayed up until the early hours. Same habits, same conversations. Occasionally I would try to think back upon the ritual, what I had done, and how I did it. I couldn't. It wasn't allowed. My mind simply forbade entry to that passage of thought.

I awoke early on a Sunday morning. I looked out of the flat window and no one was in the street. It was silent outside, not even the birds made any noise. The sun seemed dull and tired. I was exhausted for no discernible reason and so I spent the day slumped on my sofa, doing nothing at all. Hours passed, though it could have been a whole day, maybe more. I stared forward without recourse for meaning or purpose. My eyes were tired, but there was a refusal of rest. My body seized up and I was as a statue. Void of thought and memory, I looked upon the corner...

"Hell doesn't go away just because you don't like it." [XS *Rough Triangles III*]